Circus Girl Without A Name

OTHER WASHBURN BOOKS
by Wilma P. Hays

THE APRICOT TREE

THE NAUGHTY LITTLE PILGRIM

Circus Girl
Without A Name

By Wilma Pitchford Hays

Illustrated by William Ferguson

Ives Washburn, Inc. · New York

J

Ha

CIRCUS GIRL WITHOUT A NAME

Library of Congress Catalog Card Number: 71-102661

Manufactured in the United States of America

Typography by Sophie Adler

TO ROWE AND WARDY

Contents

Circus Girl Without A Name

CHAPTER ONE

Who Am I ?

With her eyes still closed, the girl awoke slowly to the sound of crying and persons talking in excited voices. Then she felt the aches in her head and her arms. She tried to see where she was. What had happened?

It was like looking through a mist, but the room seemed large. People appeared and disappeared before her like ghosts in a fog. The cot-stretcher on which she lay was barely wider than she was. Had she been in an accident? Where? When?

Her eyes cleared and she saw steel beams crossing a high ceiling, a row of bleacher seats against a wall. It couldn't be a hospital, yet there were rows of persons on army cots set up on the varnished wood floor.

1

CIRCUS GIRL WITHOUT A NAME

A uniformed nurse hurried past. A man wearing only blue jeans, his chest and arms covered with tattoo, paused to look at her, then hurried on. Another man walked toward her between the rows of cots, glancing from side to side at each face as if he, too, was searching for someone. He bent over her, his face blackened with soot and his light hair and eyebrows singed.

"Dolly," he called to a young woman behind him. "I've found Linda. Your daughter's alive."

"No, Leo. You couldn't," the woman said. "I was coming to tell you—"

The grief in her voice was so great that the girl on the cot began to cry silently, tears squeezing from the corners of her eyes.

The man who had been called Leo, stood up. She saw that he wore satin tights and a jacket which might have been white, trimmed with gold before it became blackened and charred.

"Dolly, come," he urged. "She needs you."

He drew her to the girl's side. "See, Dolly," he said. "She's about thirteen or fourteen, Linda's size, and she has blue eyes. When you can see her better, you'll recognize her."

The woman scarcely looked down, but the girl stared at her. Dolly was slender, and covered from throat to toe in pink tights crusted with pink sequins like jeweled

2

scales on a mermaid. Her dark eyes were wide open and set in shock.

Leo watched Dolly's face anxiously, hopefully. Then he saw that the girl was conscious and spoke to her. "You are Linda Vasi, aren't you?"

She was too dazed to say a word.

He tried again. "Did you have long light brown hair?"

She did not know, and she was suddenly afraid, for she could not remember even what she looked like.

"You'll recognize Linda's costume," Leo said to Dolly and turned back the blanket on the cot. He looked disappointed.

"She's wearing a hospital gown now," he said. "But whoever brought her in may remember her clothes, unless they were burned too much."

For the first time the girl saw the bandages on her hands and arms. She felt bandages around her throat and across her forehead and over her nose. She was bundled in gauze. She must have been in a fire. But where?

One thing she felt sure of: she had never seen the man or the pink lady before. She had never seen the gymnasium. She realized now that this was a school gym where so many injured persons lay on cots. Above her was a goal net for basketball and a scoreboard printed with HOME TEAM—VISITING TEAM.

"What happened?" she asked. "Did I go to a basket-ball game? Did—"

The man hurried to answer and help her recall. "Diane caught you up in her trunk," he said. "You're lucky. She brought you and your mother out safe."

Leo spoke with a slight foreign accent. Nothing he said made sense to her. She frowned. "Brought me out —in a trunk?" she said.

"The elephant's trunk," he said. "You and Dolly were ready to do your elephant act when the fire broke out in the Big Top."

"The Big Top," she said. "You mean I was at a circus?"

"Don't you know?" Leo asked in surprise. He looked at her, then at Dolly.

The pink lady was trembling. She touched the bandage on the girl's head. "What is your name?" she asked.

The girl could not answer. She did not know. She could remember nothing about her life until she opened her eyes a few moments ago. She was terrified and held out her hand to the woman.

"Tell me," she begged. "Who am I?"

"It's the shock," Leo said. "She'll remember in a little while."

"Don't be afraid," the pink lady said to her. "Some-one will find you soon."

4

A doctor hurried to the girl's side and looked in her eyes with a light. "Your daughter wasn't burned deeply," he said, "and she'll improve now that her family has found her."

"She isn't my—" Dolly began, then stopped as the girl looked at her in fear again.

Dolly turned to the doctor. "You mean she doesn't know who she is?"

"There are so many injured and dead," the doctor answered, "and many identifications were destroyed in the fire. Most of the injured were able to tell us who their relatives were. This girl's problem was complicated. She's lost her memory, only temporarily we hope."

"You mean," Dolly asked, "this child has no one to take care of her? No one to help her?"

Leo looked at Dolly as if she was the one who had lost her memory.

"She didn't have until you found her," the rushed doctor said. "I was concerned that she might have lost her entire family in the fire and the shock would add to her problem. Now she should improve rapidly."

Dolly should have been relieved but she only looked more troubled. She and Leo moved aside and talked together while the doctor completed his examination of the girl. The girl could not hear what they said until

5

Dolly's last words, "We must help her. What can I do?"

"Your daughter should be in the hospital a few days," the doctor said now, "where we can make her comfortable while her blisters heal. Just leave your name and address at the information desk. I'll see she gets into a hospital and notify you." He hurried on to the next cot.

The girl looked at the pink lady. "Am I Linda Vasi?" she asked. "Your daughter?"

Dolly Vasi went down on her knees beside the cot and put her arms gently over the girl. "Don't worry," she said, "I'll take care of you."

Again the girl was comforted by the woman's sympathy, but she was troubled, too. Dolly Vasi did not act like a mother who had just found that her daughter was alive. Her dark eyes were dazed with grief even while she tried to make the girl feel secure and safe.

"You're going to the hospital now," she said. "I won't be able to see you for a few days, but Leo will visit you."

The few days in the hospital were a busy blur to the girl. She was fed and tested and given yellow capsules to keep her sleeping much of the time. Once she woke drowsily to find Leo sitting on a chair beside her bed.

His summer sport shirt was open at the throat. Around his neck was a slender chain holding a tusk-shaped gray tooth banded in silver. She wanted to ask

6

him what it was but she was too tired to speak. He saw that she was awake.

"Dolly had to be away for a few days," he said. "She'll be back tomorrow, then, the doctor says, she can take you home and look after you there."

When Dolly and Leo came for her, the girl was sitting in a chair waiting. "I can stand alone," she said, "and the nurses walked me in the corridor."

"Great," Leo said.

Dolly helped her into a blue robe. "I thought a robe would slip on and off comfortably over your bandages," she said.

An orderly came with a wheelchair and wheeled her to the elevator, then to the door where a taxi waited.

The girl did not recognize the small trailer parked at the back of the circus lot. Dolly said that it had been her home on tour and in winter quarters for five years. It was scarcely longer than a truck including the motorized cab at the front.

"I drive it wherever we go," Dolly said.

"Don't I have a father?" the girl asked.

"My husband died two years ago," Dolly said.

The girl began to weep and was surprised at herself. Surely she must have learned to live with her loss after two years. Yet grief overcame her as if she had just lost her father.

She controlled her tears as Leo helped her up three

steps into the smallest possible living room with two chairs, a dropleaf table, and a two-burner gas cooking plate on a narrow shelf.

Two bunk beds were built against the sides with an aisle between. At the far end was a clothes closet and long mirror.

"How can you keep everything so neat and clean in this little space?" the girl marveled.

"In this space, we have to be neat to make room for us," Dolly said. She turned back the blue and white spread on one of the bunks for the girl.

"Are you hungry?" Dolly asked. "We usually eat in the circus cookhouse with the other performers, but I always kept snacks here for Linda—for you," she corrected herself hurriedly.

"I'll go now," Leo said. "Call me if you need anything."

Dolly said as he went to the door. "Thank you so much for everything. I don't know what I'd have done this last week without you."

The girl sat at the small table while Dolly helped her drink a glass of milk and eat slices from a fresh pear.

"What should I call Leo?" she asked. "Is he a relative?"

"Leo Bartock is an old friend," Dolly said. "He and my husband had an act together. But for the last two years Leo has worked alone in Europe, until he joined this circus a few weeks ago. Call him Leo as everyone does."

"What is his act?" the girl asked.

"He's a cat man," Dolly said. "He trains tigers, owns his own act. Most animal trainers do. He can move from circus to circus as he pleases. It won't be hard for him to find another job."

"Is he going to leave this circus?" the girl asked, for she liked Leo.

Dolly's eyes filled with tears. She could not speak for a moment, then she said, "The circus lost so many performers and animals, it is breaking up for the season. We all have to find new jobs."

The girl wanted to know a great deal more about the fire but she saw how upset and grief-stricken Dolly was when she talked about it, so she asked no more questions. She watched Dolly wash her hands in a wash basin, and then pour the water in a pail.

"We can't have plumbing," Dolly said, "when the circus moves to a new town every day."

"How do we get along without a bathroom?" the girl asked.

"We share portable rest rooms which the circus puts up at every stop. Only you will bathe here in a bucket so I can heat the water—as I did for—." She stopped and her eyes filled with tears again. "You don't remember a thing, do you?" she asked.

The girl shook her head. She wished she could remember this pretty dark-haired woman who was so kind to her. But even without makeup and the pink tights, Dolly Vasi seemed a stranger. Wearing lemon-color slacks and matching blouse, Dolly might have been her older sister. She could not think of her as "Mother."

"Is it all right," she asked, "if I call you Dolly, the way everyone else does? Just until I get used to—"

"Call me what's easiest for you," the woman said gently.

During the next ten days Dolly saw that the girl had plenty of rest and good food which she cooked on the two gas burners. Each time the doctor came, he seemed more pleased with the girl's progress. Finally he cut the dressings from her face, hands and arms, and said she had healed without scars. Her singed hair had been clipped and was growing in brown soft curls which covered her head like a boy's.

"You'll soon be able to travel," the doctor told her.

"My skin is as red as a boiled lobster," the girl said, "but I feel strong enough to go now."

"In a few days, perhaps," the doctor said. "We'll see."

"I know I could go now," she insisted.

Dolly looked at the girl's pouting face in surprise, then smiled. "I know. You don't want Leo to leave in the morning ahead of us," she said. "I've asked him here to supper. You can tell him goodbye and celebrate our new jobs."

Leo was going with another circus touring the midwest for the remainder of the season. The circus manager had agreed to hire Dolly, too.

The doctor left and Dolly went to buy groceries. The girl decided to surprise her and dress for the first time. She was tired of wearing the blue robe which slipped on and off comfortably over her bandages.

She opened the door of the closet marked "L" and looked at the clothes hanging there; three blue dresses, a red, and a white. She frowned. Yellow was her favorite color. Why did she have so much blue? She took the dresses off the rod one by one. They all seemed small, had she grown that much in the hospital? Perhaps she could find her shorts and blouses some place.

She saw a row of drawers at one end of the closet. Two of these had blue handles. They must be hers. She opened a drawer and took from it a pair of blue shorts and matching blouse.

The blouse fit, but she had to tug to get the shorts on. She pulled in her waist and buttoned the band. She was looking in the small door mirror when Dolly and Leo came in with the groceries for supper.

"All that good food," she wailed. "I don't think I can sit down in my shorts."

Dolly turned pale and leaned against the table as if

she needed support. Leo looked at her strangely. Then he said, "No exercise; when you begin working with the elephants your clothes will fit."

He spoke with a false encouragement, the girl thought. There was something very wrong, too, in the way Dolly was trembling. The girl was suddenly frightened as she had been when she waked in the gymnasium and asked, "Who am I?"

From the moment Dolly had said, "Don't worry, I'll take care of you," it had not troubled the girl too much that she had no memory of her life before the fire. For awhile she was content just to know that she belonged with Dolly. She had not forgotten the ordinary skills, how to read and write and speak. But she did not remember a thing about the circus or elephants.

"Was I good in the act?" she asked anxiously. "Will I know what to do? Right now I'm scared to death at the thought of an elephant catching me up in its trunk, the way you said the elephant did to save me."

Neither of them answered for what seemed like a long time. Then Dolly took a deep breath and put down the bag of groceries. She held a bunch of celery in both hands, tightly, as if it were a wand that could give her strength.

"I've never really called you Linda," Dolly said. "Have I?"

"No," the girl said slowly.

"You are not Linda."

"Not Linda?" the girl said. "Then where is she?"

"The elephant brought her from the Big-Top," Dolly said, "but Linda was dead from the smoke."

"Then who am I?" the girl cried. "How did I escape?"

Dolly shook her head, unable to answer. Her dark eyes were wide with grief as they had been the night she found the girl.

Leo's voice was filled with sympathy for both of them. "I wish we knew who you are," he said. "I thought you were Linda when I called Dolly to your cot. Wrapped in bandages, you looked like Linda, that's why I said the elephant brought you out. But Dolly knew that her daughter died in the fire."

"Someone must have been at the circus with me," the girl said. "Someone must have helped me."

"You were one of the many children Father Kelly rescued," Leo answered. "But Father doesn't know who you are."

"I was a stranger, yet you've been so good to me!" the girl said to Dolly. "It must have been awful for you, trying to cover your grief for my sake."

Dolly recovered her composure. She came and put an arm around the girl's shoulders. "At first I pretended

13

you were my own daughter only to comfort you, until some of your own family found and claimed you. I thought it would only be for a few days."

"The Hartford Police Force is trying to help you," Leo said, "but no one of your description is on its list of missing persons. The police have told us they will get in touch with us at once if they do have an inquiry or discover your identity."

"When you were ready to leave the hospital," Dolly explained, "the doctor and Leo and I discussed what was best for you. We had told the doctor that you were not my daughter, that I had been touched by your helplessness, that I wanted to do for you what I hoped another woman would have done for Linda if she had been in your place."

Dolly could not go on, and Leo spoke for her. "The doctor said that you might recover more quickly if we did not tell you for awhile. He said loss of memory sometimes happens following an accident or severe shock. Then some word or sight or sound may touch the memory and bring the past back to you all at once. Or you may remember slowly, bit by bit, snatches of the past—until, finally—"

"But I will remember?" the girl cried. All at once she was filled with panic that she did not know her name, where she came from or, anything about herself.

"The doctor thinks you will," Leo said, "if you can

live without anxiety, with someone who cares about you."

"That's why we decided to let you think you were Linda—for awhile," Dolly said, "to give you a chance to become stronger. But now you have a right to know."

The girl did not know what to say. She was suddenly overwhelmed by the kindness of these two strangers who had done so much for her, particularly Dolly who had hidden her grief at the loss of her own daughter, to help a girl she had never seen before. She must have attended to Linda's funeral while she was in the hospital.

"I'm sorry, so sorry about Linda," she said finally.

"I know," was all Dolly could say.

Leo said, "We dreaded to tell you. But now that you know, you can make your choice."

"Choice?" she asked. And sat down on her bunk with Dolly beside her.

Leo opened three cokes and handed a bottle to each of them. Then he said, "The state would assume responsibility for you, I think. Though actually they have no way of knowing whether you are a Connecticut resident or from another state."

"You mean—put me in an orphans' home?" the girl said.

"A foster home," Dolly said quickly. "But we have talked to Father Kelly, too. He's a priest here who loves

15

the circus people and visits us every year. Father said the nuns at St. John's School will look after you, if you want to stay here."

The girl said nothing. They wanted to be rid of her, and she had thought they liked her as much as she liked them.

"Of course there's a third choice," Dolly said. "To go with us on tour with the Circus."

The girl caught Dolly's hand in both of hers. "I want to go with you. You know I do."

Dolly smiled, and Leo teased. "I thought you were scared to death of riding in an elephant's trunk."

"She doesn't have to," Dolly said.

"But I want to learn the elephant act," the girl said. "I do. I won't be as good as Linda—but it's a way of showing how grateful I am that you are helping me."

"I'll teach you as soon as you are stronger," Dolly said.

Supper seemed like a celebration. But that night when Leo had gone and she and Dolly lay in their bunks in the dark, the girl thought, I feel as happy as if my problem was solved, while, actually it is just beginning. Until tonight, I thought I knew who I was and had only to remember. Now, I don't remember and I don't know who I am, either.

She lay awake a long time, drifting in and out of sleep. Dolly seemed unable to sleep well, either, and finally said, "I guess you'll have to choose a name. What shall we call you?"

The girl was not quite asleep, only floating on the edge of it and the name came easily into her mind. "Margie," she said. "My name is Margie."

Dolly answered quickly, sharply. "Margie what? What is your last name?"

"Just Margie," she answered, a little impatiently, for she was very sleepy now, exhausted with the discovery of something that had been troubling her for a long time and, now, was settled.

CHAPTER TWO

Red Cunningham

Sitting in the high seat of the trailer's cab beside Dolly, Margie watched the countryside, fascinated by the many changes of scene as they drove along the Connecticut turnpike, through the fringe of New York City, over the George Washington Bridge, the Jersey Turnpike, through the wooded mountains and tunnels of Pennsylvania, into wide open spaces. They passed fields, and farms with huge barns before they stopped to eat a picnic lunch at a roadside table.

Dolly stretched her arms above her head, "Oh, my aching shoulders," she said. "We've been on the road seven hours and still two hundred miles to reach the circus grounds tonight."

"I wish I were old enough to help with the driving,"

Margie said. "I don't even know if I've learned to drive."

"You did remember for a moment the other night," Dolly said unwrapping their sandwiches. "You said, 'My name is Margie' with such conviction, I feel sure that *is* your real name."

"Yes," Margie said, "the name came to me automatically when you asked, but that's all I remember."

"More will come to you," Dolly comforted her. "The doctor said you might remember in little snatches, at first, or a burst of memory may come at one time. Besides, Father Kelly or the Hartford Police may discover who you are—so don't be troubled. Enjoy your new experiences and wait and trust."

"I will," Margie said. "I really will."

When they reached Minola, Ohio where the Carter-Cunningham Circus was playing, strings of unshaded light bulbs, strung over the set-up, guided them to the circus grounds. The Saturday night performance was just over when Dolly drove into the alfalfa stubble behind the Big Top. Here the living tents and trailers of the performers were set up in a row.

"This is a part of the circus the public doesn't see," Dolly said. "The backyard where we live."

"It looks like a street in a small town," Margie said, "with tents and trailers instead of houses. Even folding lawn chairs beside the doors."

"We try to set up in the same way wherever we go," Dolly said. "When we move to another town every night or two, we like to feel at home in the backyard."

Leo must have been watching for them. Still wearing his white satin performer's cape, he waved them toward a vacant spot in the field.

"You must be tired," he said when he reached them. "Let me back the trailer in for you."

In minutes the trailer was lined up with the tents and they were home. Leo stepped from the cab.

"No performance tomorrow, Sunday," he said. "And we won't move on until afternoon. Only a short run to our next town."

"My aching shoulders," Dolly groaned. "I'm going to sleep until noon."

Leo smiled. "Sleep late, then I'll take you to meet the elephants," he said. "This circus has only five. Two of them aren't bad. You'll be able to work out your act all right."

When Dolly and Margie were lying in their bunks with only the aisle between, the girl asked. "You had lots more elephants before, didn't you?"

"Yes, more than twenty when we were working with Ringling."

"What did Leo mean when he said that two of the elephants weren't bad, and could do your act?"

"Some elephants are quicker to learn than others, like

20

people," Dolly said. "And some are ugly-tempered or lazy. I hope there's at least one elephant with a good disposition and dependable. A real performer who reacts to an audience."

"Wouldn't it be easier if you owned your own elephants, like Leo owns his tigers?" Margie asked.

Dolly laughed. "An elephant costs thousands of dollars and weighs tons. I don't think we'd find it easy to pull her behind our trailer either."

Margie grinned at the picture that came into her mind. "I guess not," she said, "but wouldn't it be fun to see the stares of all the people who passed us on the highway?"

Dolly was still asleep when the sun waked Margie. She slipped out of bed and pulled on the new yellow shorts and shirt and a pair of sneakers Dolly had bought for her. There was no reason why she shouldn't see for herself the kind of life she was going to live from now on, at least until someone claimed her or she remembered who she was.

There was not a person in the big backyard. Even the animals were quiet as if they knew few performers were up early today. At the far end of the row of animal shelters were the tigers' cages. At the other end, a tent for the ponies and horses with a training circle beside it.

In the center stood the biggest tent in the row, almost half as wide as the Big Top itself, although much lower. It had to be the elephants' tent.

Margie ran toward it. When she heard the tramp of enormous feet on the earth, she slowed and cautiously approached the entrance in the weather-stained canvas. She stood in the doorway to let her eyes adjust to the dark interior.

Her heartbeat quickened as she looked at the huge gray jungle creatures chained by a back leg to iron stakes as thick as a tree limb. Snakelike trunks swayed from side to side. Wide ears lifted like enormous fans on the sides of heads. Margie wrinkled her nose at the odor of the closed tent.

"You don't like—get out," a voice hissed at her.

She saw a little man standing beside one of the elephants. He was scarcely larger than she, with a soiled striped turban wrapped high on his head to make him appear taller. His nutbrown skin was as wrinkled as the elephant's hide and he wore only a faded pair of dungarees cut off at the knees.

What a freak, Margie thought. She jumped when he shouted at her.

"I not freak—even if I not look like you!"

Had he read her mind or was the thought plain to see in her face? She backed away as he came toward her shaking a skinny finger.

"Towners not allowed in circus backyard," he

warned. "No got good sense. Come sudden—scare elephants. Then if elephant kill—elephant to blame!"

He was so scornful and angry that Margie turned and ran. She bumped into a boy who was coming along the row of tents. He called, "Ouch," and caught his jaw where her head struck him.

"I'm sorry," she said. "He—he frightened me. The brown dwarf."

The boy smiled. He seemed a year or two older than Margie with the reddest shock of hair she had ever seen. If he had the freckles to go with it, his skin was too tanned to show them.

"You mean Toomai?" he said. "He's no dwarf. He's the best elephant man we have, our trainer, came here from India where he grew up working with elephants."

"Toomai's an odd name," Margie said.

"I don't know his Indian name," the boy said. "We call him Toomai, after Toomai of the Elephants in Kipling's *Jungle Books.*"

"I should have remembered," Margie said.

"I'm not doing so well myself," he said. "I should have introduced myself, I'm Red Cunningham. I walk the tightwire. All my family does. But I don't need to tell you that circus families usually work out an act together. You must be the new girl with the Vasi elephant act."

He stopped and looked at her admiringly. "You

W. FERGUSON

24

must be good to take Linda Vasi's place. *Billboard* says Linda was a star in her own right—nearly as good as her mother."

Margie didn't know what to say. Was she expected to be a star performer?

"I don't know whether I'll be good or not," she confessed. "I don't know elephants as Linda Vasi did. It's all—so new to me that I—."

Red saw her confusion and spoke gently, "I'm sorry about Linda. I read about the fire in *Billboard*."

Margie looked puzzled. "*Billboard?*" she asked.

"You must know the showman's magazine," Red said. "I was in last year myself, with my father of course, in a writeup about our family type of circus that had held together for three generations."

Red Cunningham, Margie thought. CARTER AND CUNNINGHAM CIRCUS.

"Your father is one of the owners?" she asked.

"And the hardest worker among us," Red said. "Walks tightwire. Keeps an eye on everyone and everything. Sells tickets if the help quits or gets drunk. Ballyhoos. You name it, Dad does it."

He grinned. "I'm starved. You had breakfast?"

Margie shook her head. Usually she had no trouble finding something to say but this breezy, friendly Red Cunningham didn't give her much chance to get a word in.

"Come to the cookhouse," he said. "On Sundays we have pancakes and bacon and eggs." He placed a hand on his stomach and drew in his muscles to indicate that he was hollow and caved in.

"Me, too," Margie said and went with him.

The cookhouse was a long tent divided down the center by an aisle which ended at the kitchen area where a dark-skinned cook was turning pancakes on a sizzling griddle.

"Good morning, Seth," Red said and held out two plates to be filled with bacon, eggs and pancakes.

"We sit here on the performers' side," Red told Margie, turning to the right.

She could see no difference between the wooden tables and benches on either side. Except that on the left, two dozen men in work clothes were already eating, while she and Red were the only ones at the tables on the performers' side.

Red went to get two glasses of milk, then gave his attention to his breakfast. The food was delicious but Margie was too curious to eat without interruption.

"I don't see why that little man, Toomai, was so angry with me," she said. "He called me a towner."

"Because town people often take chances with animals that circus people would never risk," Red said. "You probably startled Toomai, and you could have

26

startled the elephants, too. You must have seen what an elephant can do if it goes on a rampage."

"No," Margie admitted. "I've a lot to learn, I'm afraid. But I'll learn." She had just met Red, but she liked him. She could not bring herself to tell him that she had lost her memory. There was nothing shameful about it but she was suddenly shy and disturbed about discussing it until she knew him better.

"The elephants were chained," she said. "They seemed safe enough."

"The elephants have been trained to stay in those chains," he said, "but if a bull decided to break loose, there isn't a chain or stake strong enough to hold her."

"Her?" Margie said.

He laughed. "An elephant is always called a bull, even though we use only females in the circus. Females are easier to handle. But why am I telling you this? You're the elephant girl."

Margie finished her breakfast thoughtfully. How little she knew of circus life. She had not dreamed that so much would be expected of her. She had tried to tell Red how little she knew, but he seemed unable to understand that she didn't even like to be near the big jungle beasts. He assumed that she must know something about the circus.

"Red," she began, but was interrupted by a family of

performers who came into the dining tent and sat at
the next table. These men and women would overhear
her if she said, I don't know a thing about elephants. I
don't even know who I am. She did not want to tell her
problem and troubles to everyone. She would wait for
the right time to tell Red about herself.

"Our elephant girl," Red said to the newcomers.
"Margie, these are the Sallendo cousins. They ride the
performing horses."

The five blond Sallendos smiled and nodded their
heads vigorously as if to make themselves understood
although they greeted her in a foreign language.

"Polish," Red said to Margie. "They joined us at the
beginning of the season. I don't think they understand
any English except 'ice-cream' and 'thank-you'."

Then they would not have known what I was about
to say, Margie thought.

"I guess most circuses are kind of international," Red
said. "My father's Scotch-Irish, but my mother is Hun-
garian like Dolly Vasi. And Leo's from Belgium. You
look English with maybe a little French."

Now was the time to say she did not know what she
was. But they had finished eating and Red stood up.
They left the cookhouse together.

"I've got to practice," Red said. "See you around."

Margie stood where she was for a moment, relieved
that she didn't have to tell Red, right now, of her prob-

lem. She felt that Red liked her. Would he be as interested if he knew she was just a towner, ignorant of the circus that was his life? His act must mean a lot to him if he practiced even on Sunday morning. She would have to practice like that, work every day with the elephants, if she hoped to win for herself the admiration Red had shown for Linda's skill.

Margie heard a whip crack far down the row of animals. Leo was entering the high-fenced circle where he trained his tigers. She ran and watched him through the strong wire mesh. With a whip in one hand and an upturned chair in the other, Leo ordered four beautiful orange and black striped cats onto high stools.

Three tigers obeyed at once but the fourth cat stood in the center of the ring and snarled. Margie saw the tiger's wide open throat, larger around than a man's head, its long white teeth. It crouched and growled like rolling thunder. Even with the fence between, she wanted to run.

Leo held the chair with legs forward like a shield, and cracked his long whip on each side of the great beast. Yet he did not touch the tiger, not so much as to flick the foot-long whiskers on the sides of its snarling face.

"Stool!" he ordered, cracked his whip again and waited.

Crouching, the tiger backed a few inches at a time,

rose slowly, leaped as gracefully as a kitten onto the high stool, then sat on its haunches and glared at the man.

"Enough now, into your cages," Leo said and cracked his whip toward the gates which the cage-boy was lifting at the far side of the training circle.

The tigers raced with each other to enter. Leo followed and dropped the heavy gates. When he joined Margie, she saw beads of sweat on his forehead.

"You were wonderful," she said. "You made him mind without even touching him with the whip."

He pulled a plaid shirt over his bare brown chest and dungarees. "I intend to live longer," he said, "but I won't if I touch that tiger with a whip."

He walked beside Margie toward the living tents and trailers.

"I train and discipline my cats with patience and kindness," Leo said. "I feed them myself and stay with them as much as I can. They learn to know me and respect my orders. But if this one gets lazy or mean, I know enough not to force him too far. He's fourteen feet and eight hundred pounds of jungle tiger."

"He looks even bigger than that," Margie said. "I was really scared for a minute."

"The thing to remembr about any wild animal," Leo said, "no matter how tame they seem to be, they're savage at heart. They react quickly if they are startled.

And don't ever hurt them. With their strength and size, they don't have to take punishment from anyone!"

Leo was saying almost the same thing about tigers that Red had said about elephants, Margie thought. They obeyed from training and respect or from attachment to their masters, but the power lay in these animals to disobey if they chose. Even to kill. Performing with savage animals required much more skill and understanding than she realized.

Perhaps Leo sensed what she was thinking, for he said, "You don't have to learn the act, you know. Dolly will understand."

"Dolly has been so wonderful to me, I want to do it for her," Margie said. She did not add that she also wanted Red to admire her.

"Leo," she said, "do you think I will learn to be good with elephants? Not a star, like Linda, of course, but good enough so people will clap and cheer?" She flushed. "That sounds vain, doesn"t it?"

He smiled. "Every performer loves applause," he said. "You practice, and you'll be good enough."

CHAPTER THREE

Elephants

Sunday afternoon the circus moved in a two-hour drive to another town. The workmen set up the tents in a field so like the one before that Margie would scarcely have known there was a change except that they were close to a river now. Across a field, she could see a line of thick tall trees growing along the river's banks.

She watched Toomai and five men, each armed with a long pole tipped with a sharp hook, lead the elephants down a ramp from low box-car-sized trucks. The elephants were picketed in an outside enclosure which the men called a kraal.

The elephants tossed their heads from side to side, raised their trunks and trumpeted. Margie was frightened when they lifted their enormous ears like fans, then beat upon the ground with their trunks.

"What's the matter with them?" she asked Red as he came from his family's large blue trailer home. He was wearing bathing trunks.

"They smell the river," Red said. "They love water but usually have to be content with buckets brought to them by the bull hands. When my father rented this field from the farmer, he got permission for us to use the river. The elephants are going to have a treat."

Margie guessed that "bull hands" meant the men who looked after the elephants. "Can we watch them?" she asked.

"I'd like a swim myself," Red said. "I'm waiting for my sister, Sally. Why don't you get your suit?"

Margie ran to her trailer. When she returned wearing her yellow and white polka dot suit, Red's sister was with him.

Sally looked about eleven years old, with the nicest smile, and curly red hair that was darker than her brother's, but *she* had the freckles to go with it. She wore owl-round, dark-rimmed glasses to frame her brown eyes.

Without waiting for an introduction, she called, "Come on, Margie", and ran after the line of elephants being led toward the river by Toomai and the bull hands.

ELEPHANTS

The woods along the river bank had not been cut in years. Underbrush and vines grew in a tangled mat beneath the tall trees. Margie, Red and Sally followed the elephants as they ploughed a path through the thicket.

Margie watched the enormous wrinkled gray legs take strides that covered half a trailer length at each step, as the elephants ripped their way through undergrowth to the river. They trumpeted their pleasure as they splashed into the water.

"We'll swim up-stream from them," Red said.

The three young people ran along the river bank where green moss felt thick as a carpet under their bare feet. They came to a curve in the river-bed, and found a wide sandy bar, beside a deeper current in which to swim. And there were rocks to explore against the far bank of the river.

"This is great," Red called. He splashed into the water, Margie and Sally right behind him.

They were soon joined by more circus performers who played and swam in the water. There were the *Sallento Cousins,* a husband and wife with a dog act, a family of pony trainers, and several clowns. At some distance upstream, a woman swam alone.

Red saw Margie looking at her. "She looks like a gypsy," Margie said. "What does she do?"

Red grinned. "You'll see. Come on, I'll race you up there."

Margie flattened one cheek against the water and struck out with long fast strokes. Swimming was something she did well, she discovered. She passed Red, drew even with the lone woman and surfaced. She shook her dripping hair and blinked.

Before her a long slender log seemed to glide through the clear water. It turned a copper-color as it drew nearer Margie, then humped into double coils like ribbon candy, turned its head slowly, and looked at her with unblinking black eyes.

A great snake. Margie screamed and swam and scrambled onto the river bank, sure that she felt the cold coils upon her heels.

"He's mine," the woman called. "He won't hurt you."

Red was splashing and running to catch Margie. "It's only *Nell and her Rock Python*," he called. "He's part of her act.'

Margie turned on him. "You raced me here on purpose to scare me, Red Cunningham. Don't you come near me."

She ran on past the swimmers to reach the path the elephants had made. The huge beasts were still in the river, dipping their trunks, spraying each other like children playing.

It was growing dark under the trees. Toomai called to the elephants to move along, get back to their kraal and supper. With grunts, angry snorts and trumpeting, they obeyed their trainer's commands and plodded slowly toward the bank.

Margie hesitated, then heard Red coming, and ran down the path to be ahead of him and the elephants. She had not counted on the swiftness with which the elephants could move with Toomai and the bull hands urging them along from behind. The lead elephant was coming fast through the trees. Margie looked back over her shoulder, stumbled on a broken root and fell.

She scrambled to her feet and rubbed her scratched, stinging knees. She heard a snort behind her and turned. The lead elephant stopped and stared at her from little pig eyes that seemed to glow in the dusk.

"Get out of her way!" Red shouted. "Get behind a tree."

Margie could not move.

The elephant's trunk circled her waist, lifted her and set Margie beside the trail as lightly as if she had been a leaf. Then the elephants moved on, five enormous bulks hurrying to the fodder in their kraal.

Red reached Margie. "Why didn't you get out of her way?" he said angrily, "She might not have seen you and trampled you to death."

"I was too scared to move," she cried.

"I'm sorry," he said. "I shouldn't have played the trick on you with the python. But surely *you* know your way around elephants."

She turned and ran home. Everyone thought she loved elephants, that she knew how to work with them and understood them. She simply had to begin practicing, and gain skill and confidence to overcome her fears, if she was going to live with the circus. After she had gained more courage, she wouldn't feel so shy about admitting her ignorance.

She met Leo and Dolly coming from the cookhouse. "Was the water good?" Dolly asked.

"Yes," Margie said. She ran up the trailer steps before they could see how pale and shaken she was. She dressed and came back from the trailer and joined Leo and Dolly at the elephants' kraal.

Toomai was saying to Dolly, "Not use that Peewee— she jealous—not be trusted." He turned to an older elephant. "Lizzie is leader—she best for you. Big broad head—easy to stand on."

Dolly nodded and pointed to a third elephant. "And that one," she said, "she almost dances when she walks. She ought to work well with music."

Margie thought that the big elephant's dancing looked more like a nervous swaying rock. Until this moment all elephants had looked alike to her, huge and terrifying. Now she saw that elephants, like strange persons one has just met, can be distinguished from one another.

Lizzie was the lead elephant who had lifted Margie

from her path. She stood quietly, lifting hay in her trunk and stuffing it into her mouth. Her small pig eyes were shuttered by the longest straightest lashes Margie had ever seen.

Toomai put a hand on the shoulder of the elephant who walked with a swaying rock. "She Kate," he said. "Sometimes lazy—very smart."

"I'll use those two, Lizzie and Kate," Dolly said.

"Which one is for me?" Margie asked.

Dolly looked at her. "We'll wait until we see how they work out," she said. "There's no hurry for you to practice."

"I want to," Margie said. "Please."

"It won't hurt her," Leo said, and smiled at Margie as if he understood how mixed her feelings were, frightened but determined.

"All right," Dolly agreed. "Better have supper now, then get to bed. We'll begin first thing in the morning."

CHAPTER FOUR

Under the Big Top

After breakfast Dolly and Margie came from the cookhouse wearing faded denim shorts, T-shirts and sneakers. The backyard of a circus might look like an unpaved street in a small town, with folding porch chairs beside the living tents and clothes flapping dry on lines behind them, but these fields were no place for shoes with heels. It had rained in the night and their sneakers were muddy and slick when they stopped at the elephant kraal.

Toomai had already placed a harness strap around Lizzie's thick neck and across her forehead. In his bright-striped turban, he looked like a nut-brown statue waiting below the huge gray head. He bowed to Dolly.

"Lizzie smart. You see," he said proudly.

He ignored Margie. Toomai had never actually looked at her since the day she had come suddenly upon the elephant tent and startled him. But he seemed to know that Dolly understood and loved his dear elephants.

"Thank you, Toomai," Dolly said. She took hold of the strap at Lizzie's throat and turned to Margie. "The first thing we'll learn is how to mount."

She sounded like a teacher saying to her class; "Today we'll study the first chapter on the Civil War." But, Margie thought, my heart never raced like this in any history class. Lizzie looks twice as huge as she did last night.

"The elephant will lower her head," Dolly explained. "You catch hold of her harness strap and brace a foot against her trunk. Like this. She'll carry you up.

"Trunk, Lizzie," Dolly called.

The elephant did not move.

"I know you've done this before," Dolly said sternly and pulled on the strap. "Trunk!" she commanded.

Lizzie lowered her head and ran out her trunk like a ramp.

Dolly caught the harness strap on her forehead, set her foot into the curve of the trunk and rode up, then stepped off gracefully onto Lizzie's broad flat head.

"Trunk," she called.

Lizzie reached up and brought her down again.

"Now you try it," she said to Margie.

Margie tried to think only of how much she wanted to do this right. Dolly had been so good to her. Here was her chance to please Dolly. Margie heard the command, "Trunk," and saw the elephant lower her head. She grabbed the harness strap and braced a muddy foot on the curled trunk, started up as Lizzie lifted her.

The next thing Margie knew she was flat on her face under the elephant. She scrambled on hands and knees from between the enormous wrinkled legs.

Dolly wiped dirt from her forehead. "That's enough for today," she said.

Margie was trembling but she shook her head. "I have to learn," she said. "I can do it."

She tried again and again and again. Four times she slipped down the trunk on the way up. On the fifth try, she landed on top of Lizzie's head, not standing, but sitting straddled with heels hanging over Lizzie's huge ears. Surprised, Margie looked at her hands spread palms down on the wrinkled sand-papery hide of the elephant.

"I made it," she shouted triumphantly.

Dolly was smiling when Lizzie brought Margie down. "Now," she said, "you *have* had enough. And Lizzie and I have to practice if we are to put on an act tonight."

Toomai appeared from somewhere. "Lizzie learn fast —if only you and her," he said pointedly.

"You'll find plenty to watch when you have cleaned up," Dolly told Margie.

She went to the trailer and took a bucket bath, shivering at the cold water but she did not want to take the time to heat it on the small gas burner. She dried with a turkish towel and found a dozen aching bruises that would probably turn black and blue shortly. Her left cheek was puffy, half closing the eye above it.

Would she ever be as graceful and dainty as Dolly was on an elephant?

She dressed and went to the Big Top where she had heard workmen putting up the highwires before breakfast. In the one ring in the center, the Cunningham family was practicing a tight wire act.

Margie saw that Red looked like his slender redhaired father, but both he and Sally had dark eyes like their mother's.

The Cunningham's year-old baby girl played on a blanket spread on the grass beside the ring. The baby crawled, found a cigar stub someone had dropped into the grass, and promptly put it in her mouth. Margie shuddered, and ran to take the cigar from the baby. But Mr. Cunningham jumped to the ground, threw the cigar far away, returned the baby to the blanket, and swung back onto the high wire, all in seconds.

What a strange place to bring up a family, Margie thought, as she saw Mr. Cunningham run out to meet Mrs. Cunningham on the high wire over the center of the ring. They faced each other, arms outspread, suddenly flipped and landed on opposite sides, teetered dangerously for a moment, then ran along the wire to the platforms at each end and bowed as if there was an audience in the big tent.

Red and Sally, waiting their turns to practice, clapped and smiled at their parents. Margie felt weak as if she had almost fallen from a wire herself.

Sally saw Margie and hurried to meet her. "I hope you're not still mad at Red," she said. "He knew the Python wouldn't hurt you. It only eats once a week and Nell fed him Saturday."

"That's comforting!" Margie said. "No, I'm not mad. Will it bother you if I watch you practice?"

Mr. and Mrs. Cunningham were leaving the tent carrying the baby. Red was already on the practice platform. He beckoned to Sally. "Come on. When we get through our routine, we'll show Margie around the lot."

As he ran along the high wire, testing the feel of it, Margie saw that Red was good. Sally came out more hesitantly from her platform high above the safety net stretched below.

"Don't look down at your feet," Red called to her.

"Look straight ahead at the wire, look *where you are going*, not where you are."

Sally wasn't bad, Margie thought, as she watched them work, but she was a long way from being as good as her brother. She was several years younger, of course, but it was more than that. High-wire was something that must have been born in Red.

Practice over, they jumped into the net and bounced lightly to the grass-covered ground. Sally was saying to Red, as they joined Margie, "I DO think about what I'm doing. I think and think and think."

"Your mind has to take over completely," Red instructed his sister. He held with both hands the ends of the towel he had thrown over his bare shoulders and practice trunks. "Don't see anything, don't hear anything, don't know anything except *you* and *that wire*. When my mind's really boss like that—in command of my whole body—I can somersault across a wire from one end to the other and never miss. I know the days I can do it—and the days I can't."

He turned to Margie. "You know how it feels," he said, "when you've worked until it is exactly right. Then you can't go wrong."

Margie opened her mouth a little in amazement. Red actually looked upon his high-wire circus act as an art, instead of an odd way of making a living. When he was working on his act, it was the most important thing in the world to him.

Apparently Sally was used to her brother's intense desire for perfection. She ignored him and looked at Margie, frowning a little.

"You look so disapproving," she said.

"Oh, no," Margie said hurriedly, "I'm just not used to real—I mean boys and girls who—" she stopped. She had almost said, "Girls and boys who perform for a living," and she was horrified. How snobbish she would have sounded.

"You're not what I expected, either," Sally said. "I thought you'd be tiny like Dolly, and—"

"You're certainly not too big," Red told Margie hastily.

"I didn't mean that," Sally said. "But I thought you'd be more enthusiastic and talk about your act. Can you do the hand stand? Like Linda Vasi?"

"I—I don't remember seeing Linda's act," Margie said.

"I have a picture of it right here," Sally said. "In last month's *Billboard*." She ran to the dressing tent at one end of the Big Top and returned with the showman's magazine open to a full color photograph of the *Vasi Elephant Act*.

The picture must have been taken during a performance for there was a blur of many upturned faces in the background. Dolly rode gracefully, in a pointed toe ballet stance, on the head of the lead elephant. Her headdress was of tall pink plumes and she wore a pink spangled costume like the one she had been wearing when Margie first saw her after the circus fire.

Behind Dolly, on the head of a second elephant, a girl in blue spangles stood on her hands, her legs stretched high and close together straight as an arrow.

"Well, can you?" Sally asked impatiently.

Will I ever ride so beautifully and gracefully on an elephant? Margie thought. It is a good thing Red and Sally didn't see me practicing. I must tell them right now how little I really know.

She shook her head. "I can't do that," she began. "In fact——"

Her words were drowned by the furious barking of a little dog which ran through the Big Top as if delighted to see Red and Sally. It was the tiniest dog Margie had ever seen, scarcely larger than a tree squirrel. It danced around the young people on its pencil thin legs, and they laughed at the big noise such a small dog could make.

An older man followed, caught up the dog and cuddled it against him. "Quiet, Chica," he scolded. "That's no way to greet a guest."

Red introduced Margie to Mr. Carter. "Mr. Carter and my grandfather started this circus together," Red said. "He still keeps the account books and does a clown act with Chica."

"Yes," the old man said, "we joined up, Carter and Cunningham, fifty years ago the end of this July. We started with only five acts, I remember."

Someone called to him from the performers' entrance and the old man left.

"I thought he was going to tell you all about the 'old days'," Sally said. "When Mr. Carter gets started, you can't stop him."

"He's had a lot of interesting experiences," Red said. "Wrecks and wind and fire and flood. Once the circus was stranded in a little town on the Missouri River by a flood that took out all the approaches to the bridges. The stores ran out of food and the circus people had nothing to eat for seven days except pancakes and coffee. (That was before helicopters of course). The animals ate every bit of hay and meat in the area and were growing mean-tempered with hunger. Then Mr. Carter had an idea. He brought large ferries up the Missouri and ferried the circus across the river."

"Well," Sally said, "if Mr. Carter doesn't tell you *all*, Red will."

Her brother ignored her and said to Margie, "We

never have a season without one blow-down. But I don't need to tell you about the hazards of life on tour."

She knew then that she must tell them, now before another interruption, but how to begin? They walked from the Big Top into sunshine and stopped beside a roped ring to watch ponies practice, before Margie managed to say, "I know nothing about blow-downs, or tours. I don't know a thing about a circus or elephants."

Red was laughing at the jealous maneuvering of a spotted pony trying to push another from the sugar reward offered by their trainer. It was several seconds before he realized what Margie had said. He turned and stared at her as Sally was doing.

"Then what are you doing here?" Sally asked incredulously.

"In an elephant act?" Red added, "One of the most important acts in the circus!"

They are more than surprised, Margie thought. They're angry and I can't blame them. They are proud of their circus, and an ignorant "towner" like me can bring criticism on their show, if my work is poor.

"I'm learning the act," she said, "Dolly took me with her, for I had no place to go, unless I went to a foster home, or spent the summer with the nuns at St. Johns."

"You haven't any family?" Red asked in a kinder voice.

"I don't know," Margie said.

"Don't know?" Sally exclaimed.

"*If* I have a family," Margie answered, "surely some-one would have missed me and found me by now."

Red and Sally were looking at her as if the noon sun must be too hot on her head. She did feel a bit dizzy from the swift beating of her heart. "I don't know a thing about my past," she said. "I lost my memory after the fire."

"At Hartford, when Linda Vasi died?" Red asked.

"That's why Dolly tried to help me," Margie explained. "I was her daughter's age, and no one claimed me. She felt sorry for me and the doctor thought I might remember when I recovered from my burns and shock."

"But you haven't?" Sally asked. "Not a thing?"

"Only my first name," Margie said, "when I was almost asleep, and Dolly asked me, suddenly in the night, what she should call me."

"It must be awful," Sally said, "not to know who you are. I mean you could be a thief, or have run away from home, or—"

Red gave her a withering look and interrupted, "You'll get used to Sally's imagination running away with her," he told Margie. "I'm glad we know. There must be something we can do to help you."

Margie blinked rapidly to stop sudden tears. Were

51

all circus performers as understanding and ready to help others as Red and Dolly and Leo? Yes, and Sally, too, for the younger girl was saying, "Don't worry. We'll think of some plan. Right now Mother is waiting for us to go into town. Tomorrow's Red's birthday, and we have to buy his present and get the cake and things."

"If we don't see you before the performance tonight," Red said, "we'll see you after practice in the morning."

That evening, Margie stood against the wall of the crowded women's dressing tent behind the Big Top. What confusion and excitement! Girls, who would swing high on the ropes in the aerial act, dashed around zipping each other into stretch suits made of net and sequins. The wardrobe woman helped Dolly into a butterfly costume, pink with brightly colored markings on the gauzy wings.

Finally, Margie followed the others into the dusk of the backyard where the persons and animals were lining up outside the performers' entrance to the Big Top. There was gypsy Nell with her python coiled around an arm and neck. A juggler tossed flaming torches over his wife's head. Someone lighted a finale sparkler too soon, and the keepers had trouble holding the elephants, horses and dogs that thought the parade had begun.

Where had everyone come from? There were more than a hundred persons ready to perform or helping those who did.

The eight-piece band began to play a lively tune as curtains opened at the back of the tent. Old Mr. Carter, his face painted white with a red bulbous nose, ran first into the Big Top, chased by Chica barking furiously. At the sight of the tiny dog frightening the big clown, the children shouted, men and women laughed.

The clown stumbled and bent to catch himself. The little dog ran up his back and sat upon his head, then lifted a tuft of the man's hair as if it were reins to guide a horse. The crowd roared and clapped.

Margie smiled. Everyone was having such a good time, she, too, wanted to take part in the show.

For two hours she watched fascinated from the shadows of the performers' entrance, while act followed act in the center of the Big Top. Leo seemed as grand as a duke in his white satin suit trimmed with silver braid, his straight blond hair falling across his forehead above deepset gray eyes, when he cracked his whip and commanded his snarling tigers.

Then the electricians, crouched behind floodlights on poles at the four corners of the tent, turned their lights upward for the Cunningham's act. The vast dark dome of the tent changed to brightness now while the audience below was in shadow. Margie looked up at the

high wire, which glittered in beams of light, fragile as the thread leading to a spider's nest. She held her breath as the four Cunninghams, in brief green and gold costumes, ran gaily along the thread. High up there, they swung from one another's hands, and tumbled seemingly as care-free as children.

They are so disciplined, they make it look easy, Margie thought, But I have seen how hard they practice. Surely anything I have to learn to do on an elephant can't be as dangerous as the acts Red and Sally are performing.

In the finale, Dolly rode Lizzie around the entire floor of the Big Top, with lights low. Only a spotlight followed and turned her butterfly costume into a thousand sparkling colors.

Lizzie stopped in the center of the ring, stood on her hind legs, wound her trunk around Dolly's slim legs and lifted her high. Dolly leaned far out to the audience, opened her arms and spread her glittering wings.

Margie heard the people draw in a common breath at the beautiful sight. She caught her hands before her.

"I'll do that, too, before the season is over," she told herself. "I will."

CHAPTER FIVE

Red's Birthday

Margie was up early the next morning. She made more noise than usual as she washed and dressed, hoping that Dolly would wake, too. With the daily moves the circus made, and Dolly's own practice for her act, there was scarcely more than an hour each morning for Margie to train. She was anxious to get to work, but Dolly continued to sleep, her head half buried under a pillow.

Margie went to the cookhouse and found Leo eating, the only person on the performers' side. He smiled and beckoned her to join him. When they finished breakfast, he said, "I'm training the cubs now. Want to watch until Dolly's ready?"

She walked with him past the rows of animal tents

toward the tiger cages. One of the cage-boys was raking the floor of an empty cage with a long cleaning bar. Leo knelt before another cage where a nervous mother tiger paced back and forth followed by two nursing-age cubs.

Leo tossed a few scraps of raw meat into the empty cage which joined the cage of the mother tiger. With a hook he lifted the door between the two. The big tiger sprang through the opening to eat the meat. Leo dropped the door between the cages.

"Now," he said to Margie, "we can get the cubs."

He lifted a baby tiger, no bigger than a small dog, and held it in his lap. The cub arched its orange-and-black-striped back, bared its teeth and snarled as fearlessly as if it were full-size.

"He's so cute," Margie said. "Will he bite?"

"Sure," Leo said, "and his teeth are sharp. But I have to start training him early, the earlier the better for a dangerous act."

He began to stroke the cub's head between its little cat ears. Soon the cub pushed against him and rolled on its side. Gently Leo pried open the cub's mouth and laid his wrist between the two rows of fangs.

The cub closed its teeth on his bare flesh. Leo talked gently to it. "Easy, that's enough."

The cub pressed its teeth deeper, watching Leo through golden cat-slit eyes. Leo cuffed him sharply as

a mother cat cuffs her kittens when they play with her too roughly.

The cub laid back its ears and whined, but it loosed its grip. Margie saw the white dent its teeth had made in Leo's flesh.

"Why do you give him a chance to bite you?" she asked.

"In a couple of years," Leo said, "I'll be putting my head in his mouth before an audience. I can't start too young to train him for *that*."

Margie shivered, seeing the bared fangs of the mother tiger who had eaten the meat and was pacing back and forth, snarling and flinging herself against the bars to reach her cubs. Leo returned the little one to its cage and lifted the door for its mother.

Margie watched her lick the two mewing cubs, tumbling them off their feet with her big pink tongue. The sun was warm on her head and she felt a moment's dizziness. Then she turned to Leo with a sudden smile.

"My cat, Fluffy, washed her kittens like that—."

She stopped. Leo was looking at her in excitement.

"Go on," he said.

"I—don't remember anything else," she said, excited herself now. For a moment her memory had brought her a picture. In her mind she had seen her fluffy cat with kittens playing on a big bed with a white and yellow spread. Where had she had a bed like that, so different from the bunk in the trailer?

"Ready for work?" Dolly called from the elephants' kraal.

Margie ran to meet her. "I remembered again," she told Dolly.

"What?" Dolly asked quickly.

"Not anything to help," Margie admitted. "Just my gray cat with kittens, on a bed with a yellow and white spread."

Dolly seemed unusually pale. Was it because she was afraid of cats, Margie wondered, knowing that Dolly had this phobia. It seemed odd enough that Dolly, who would let an elephant scrunch down over her, trembled if a stray kitten rubbed against her ankles. It was even more strange for her to look so stricken at the mention of a kitten. Perhaps she was disturbed that I remembered so little.

"It was only for a second," Margie said, "like a door opened, then closed before I caught more than a glimpse into my room."

Dolly gave her a quick hug. "It's coming. You'll remember one day. Let's forget about it now and get to work."

She actually seemed relieved, Margie thought. Has Dolly begun to like me as much as I like her? Does she hope I will be staying with her for a long time? I hope so, too. I like the friendliness and kindliness of the performers in the circus. It's exciting to move, to see new country every day, to hear people clapping when the acts begin. But I want to earn my own way.

When today's practice was over, Margie could ride cradled in Lizzie's trunk, then step off cautiously on her wide flat head.

"Fine," Dolly said, "now you're ready to ride in the finale parade. An act can come later."

Toomai, who was always hovering near his beloved elephants, said disapprovingly: "Lizzie always *led* elephants in finale parade."

"Then," Dolly said. "Margie will ride Lizzie and carry the flag."

The Carter-Cunningham Circus ended each performance by playing the Star-Spangled Banner while the audience stood and sang with the band. Margie knew she ought to be able to ride in the curve of Lizzie's trunk and hold a flag, but there was a knot in her stomach. She could not tell whether it was excitement or apprehension.

"We'll ask wardrobe to make you a red, white and blue costume," Dolly said, "and a matching striped satin blanket for Lizzie."

"You've been doing your act with Lizzie," Margie said.

"I'll use Kate," Dolly said.

Toomai protested. "Kate balk sometimes. Lizzie is leader. Number one lady should ride boss elephant."

Margie was troubled. "He's right," she said. "You're giving Lizzie to me because she is older and dependable. You don't know how that skitterish Kate might act."

"Skitterish!" Dolly repeated and laughed.

Margie had to smile, too, at the idea that anything as

enormous and strong as an elephant could be skitterish. But the restless Kate had always seemed nervous to her.

"I've decided to use Kate," Dolly said, "because she's younger and gets down on her knees, and up again, more easily than Lizzie can. Besides, Kate's the biggest, and the audience feels greater suspense when Kate scrunches down on all fours over me."

Dolly spread a small rug under Kate's belly and lay down on it, face up between the huge rocking front legs.

"Kneel," she ordered.

Kate trumpeted, lifted her wide fan ears and stood as she was.

"Kneel," Dolly called again.

Kate swung her trunk back and forth and snorted.

"Get out, please," Margie called. "She looks mean."

Dolly rolled from under the stubborn Kate. "You know what I want," she scolded the elephant. "You did it well yesterday. We'll try again."

Before she could slide under Kate, Toomai said something to Lizzie in his Indian tongue. The old elephant moved quickly and began spanking Kate with her trunk as an exasperated mother might punish an unruly child. Kate squealed and fell on her knees, then rose again at Dolly's command.

This time there was no nonsense from Kate when

Dolly lay down under her pillar-like legs and ordered her to kneel.

Lizzie walked calmly to Toomai and held out her trunk. He gave her the peanuts she expected as reward, and nodded his turbaned head.

"Kate remember now that Lizzie is boss elephant here," he said.

"Try Lizzie again," Dolly said to Margie, "giving your own commands."

Margie tried to imitate Dolly's firm voice. "Trunk, Lizzie," she called.

The old elephant lifted her long straight lashes and gave Margie a bored tolerant look. With the end of her trunk, she investigated the peanut hulls on the ground to see if she might have missed a nut. Finding none, she reached out lazily, curved her trunk around Margie's waist and tossed the girl gently onto her head.

From her high perch, Margie saw Red and Sally coming toward the kraal and waved. They would see how much she had learned. "I'm going to carry the flag in the finale parade," she said as they stopped and looked up at her.

Lizzie moved unexpectedly. Margie lost her balance, slid down the elephant's side, until she caught its knee, and clung.

"Let go," Red said in a tone of disgust. "Your feet are only six inches from the ground."

Margie rubbed her smarting legs where the sand-papery hide had scratched her. "Anyone can have an accident," she said.

"Sure," Red said.

But Margie saw how he and Sally looked at each other. She flushed. She had wanted, so much, to be good the first time they saw her on an elephant.

"We've finished practice," Red said, "Come over and watch the Sallendos ride. Are they good!"

Margie knew Red and Sally wanted to talk to her, so she walked across the dusty grass with them.

"I've been thinking," Sally began. "If someone does claim you, later, they might have Dolly arrested for taking you."

"Sally," Red groaned. "You are too much!"

"You mean kidnapping?" Margie asked, "Surely any-one can see how good Dolly and Leo have been to me. They never saw me before, yet they paid my hospital bills, and took me with them because I needed them."

"The police might think that Dolly needed you—for her act," Sally reasoned.

"Leo talked to the police about me. I'm not on their list of missing persons. They know they can find me through Father Kelly."

"Father Kelly?" Red asked. "Everyone in the circus knows him. He's a real friend."

"His father was a trick horse trainer," Sally added, "so Father Kelly has always known performers."

"He's known Dolly for a long time," Margie said. "She wrote to tell him how much stronger I am and I saw a letter from him in the mail only yesterday."

"If Father Kelly or the police haven't had an inquiry about you," Red said, "then you really must have been a stranger in Hartford."

"That blows your plan," Sally said to her brother.

"What plan?" Margie asked.

"Red got a camera for his birthday," Sally said. "He's fifteen today."

"Happy birthday," Margie said, belatedly.

"I was going to take your picture," Red said, "and send it to a Hartford newspaper."

"Under the picture," Sally added, "Red was going to write: 'Circus Mystery Girl! Anyone know her?' "

"But there were dozens of pictures in the paper at the time of the fire," Margie said, "of the people and animals and burned tents."

"Who would recognize you wrapped in bandages?" Red asked.

"I suppose you're right," Margie agreed.

"You sound so doubtful," Sally said. "Don't you *want* to be found?"

Margie wasn't sure that she did. She had grown to love Dolly, and Leo, too. They seemed to love her. Until she traveled with the circus, she had not known how big her own country was or how beautiful. And she enjoyed being friends with Red and Sally.

"Of course I wouldn't want to worry my real family —if I have a family," she said. "But if anyone really cared what happened to me, wouldn't someone be looking for me? Or have gone to the police by now?"

"You'd think so," Sally said. "Even if you had no family, you must have had neighbors, kids you played with. They'd miss you."

"I know someone who'll be looking for you when the summer is over," Red said. "You went to school some place. If we haven't found who you are by September, your truant officer will hunt for you."

He was grinning, to make her feel better. "During the school year, Sally and I have to study every day with a tutor even when we are working on tour. When we're in winter headquarters, we attend classes in the public school and take exams every spring to prove we know as much as other kids in our grades. We can't escape school even in the circus."

"We have to run and get dressed," Sally interrupted.

They had been so interested in their discussion that they had not noticed when the other performers went to the cookhouse for lunch.

"I better be there to cut my own cake!" Red exclaimed.

"His birthday cake is five layers high," Sally said hurrying toward the trailers with Margie. "Everyone gets a piece of it."

"Be with you in a minute," Margie said, and ran to change into a yellow dress Dolly had bought for her.

Margie could hear many voices singing "Happy Birthday To You", before she reached the cookhouse. She joined in the song as she looked for a place at a table. Nell, the snake charmer, made room for her on a bench between Nell and an older man whom Margie had not met. Red was cutting his birthday cake at the Cunningham family table. Sally and her mother passed it on platters to the others.

"I never saw so many performers eating at one time before," Margie said.

Nell smiled. "We are artists, we of the circus. Each has work to take our time. We cannot keep to schedules—but to celebrate specially, a boy's birthday, we are all one family. You understand?"

Margie nodded. There was a warm friendliness here in this room which she had never felt in a crowd at any other place. Suddenly she wanted to cry, which would be ridiculous in the midst of this happy group.

The older man on her left looked down at her. "And we are all one family, when another needs help," he said gently as if he sensed her mood. "Not that we ask questions about the life of another—"

"I guess it is the music," Margie said for the small band had begun to play "He's a jolly good fellow". It gave her time to bring back her smile.

"Yes, music has strange powers," the old man agreed, when the band players stopped and he could be heard. "It can sooth or arouse courage. At the Hartford fire last month, Merle Evans saved many lives with his music. I saw—"

"You were there, at the Hartford fire?" Margie interrupted.

"Yes, I worked with Ringling for twenty years," he said. "And I never heard Merle Evans' band play better than it did that day, with the fire getting closer and closer."

Margie could almost feel the heat around her. Her throat tightened. She had never talked about the fire with Dolly and Leo, for it seemed cruel to ask Dolly to describe losing Linda. And they must have thought that such discussion would be too difficult for her. Yet, maybe if she knew what really happened that day—.

"Tell me about it?" she asked.

He did not seem to find her request strange, although everyone else at the tables was laughing and talking and eating cake and ice cream. He answered as if he had told the story many times before and knew it by heart.

"Hartford was always a good show town," he said, "but the Big Top was really packed that day with 12,000 people."

Red and Sally had left their table to find Margie, but

neither of them said a word when they heard what the old man was saying. They sat down on a bench which departing performers had vacated.

"The fire chief closed the ticket office right after we seated a hundred orphans from a children's home," he said.

"When Merle Evans' band began to play, 'Strike Up The Band,' about ten thousand kids craned their necks to see the back of the tent where the thirty musicans were seated. The kids had been chattering louder than a flock of blackbirds, but the music hushed them and the show began."

"The band played softly while the big cats jumped through wheels of fire, and snarled at their trainer's cracking whip."

Like Leo, Margie thought.

"Then everyone was laughing at the polar bears standing on their hind legs to drink from nursing bottles.

"After the cage doors clanged shut on the animals, and the cagemen were wheeling them out, a spotlight turned way up in the peak of the big-top to show the great Wallenda family on the high wire."

Margie glanced at Red and Sally who were listening as intently as she was.

"The band quit playing. There wasn't a sound from that big audience. Everyone was holding his breath at the Wallendas' thrilling finish, three high on bicycles on a thin silver thread way up there—.

"Suddenly I saw a little patch of light in the top at the far end near the Menagerie entrance. I yelled 'Fire! The Big Top's afire.' Only those near me heard above the clapping and shouts for Helen Wallenda who was coming down the rope ladder.

"Then everyone saw the flames at once, and rushed from their seats, filling the aisles, spilling into the arena, jamming the exits, crushing against the last cages.

"Merle Evans and his band didn't run. He kept them playing, trying to bring order into the panic. Even when the air was black with smoke and the tent poles were falling around them, the men stood up on the bandstand and played. In ten minutes, the heat was so intense some of the musicans had to drop their instruments. Then Merle Evans called, 'Coda', to cut, and the men jumped down and ran for the outdoors."

"Several bodies are still unidentified," he added.

The old man stopped and seemed a little dazed as if his memories were too much for him. One of the Sallendo cousins called from the door, "Come on, Pop. You haven't seen our horses yet."

Margie, Red and Sally did not move until after the man left. Then Sally said, "I knew it was awful, but not *that* bad. Mrs. Wallenda was knocked unconscious in the crush, you know. Her husband dropped down the ropes above her, got her over his shoulder and climbed and ran along the top of the chutes, then dropped over behind the grandstand. That was in the newspapers."

"It can't happen again," Red said. "Not with all the new safety rules circuses have adopted. Papa's always used fire-proofed canvas. And he'd discharge anyone who smoked near a tent or hay."

"Who was that man?" Margie asked. "The one we just talked to?"

"A friend of the Sallendos, visiting for the day," Red answered. "He's on his way home to Florida—in the Sarasota-Venice area where Ringling has its winter headquarters. It'll take awhile to build up acts and get Ringling on the road again."

"Maybe you're one of the hundred orphans," Sally said to Margie, "from the children's home he mentioned."

"No," Margie answered. "A children's home would have records. The matron would be sure to go to the police if a child was missing."

"Now that we know more of what happened," Red said, "it doesn't seem so strange that you haven't been claimed by someone. All those people—probably ten thousand children. You could have lost your entire family there—"

"Or your family could have identified the wrong

girl," Sally added, "and think you are no longer living."

"I don't know," Margie said. "I can't remember anything about that day."

"That settles it," Red said. "I'll take your picture and send it to the newspaper. I have enough birthday money to pay for an ad."

He was carrying his camera since he had taken some pictures at his birthday dinner. Outside the cookhouse, he added. "Stand here where the light is best."

Margie faced the sun while he snapped three shots to be sure one of them would be good.

"Now," Red said, winding the film, "I'll send this roll to be developed. We can pick up the pictures in care of general delivery in one of the towns we'll play. It takes about a week to get the pictures back. Where will we be then?"

He named towns on his fingers. "To be safe, I'll have them sent to Lima, Wisconsin where we'll be in eight days."

Margie was grateful that Red was trying to help her, but she was frightened, too. Was she afraid of what she might learn about herself, she wondered.

CHAPTER SIX

Blow Down

"We're lucky the circus lot is close to town here," Red said as he and Margie walked down the main street of Lima, Wisconsin, to the post office.

He asked for the circus mail at the general delivery window and the postal clerk handed him a yellow envelope with the snapshots. He spread the pictures on the wall desk.

"They're not bad," Margie said, "but I can never look at the sun without squinting".

"This one's clear," Red said, choosing a snapshot and putting it into an addressed, stamped envelope with the advertisement they had prepared earlier. He dropped it in the outgoing mail slot.

Quickly they went outdoors, where the sun made

rainbow colors of the early morning mist it was burning away.

"Nothing to do now but wait," Red told her, "and we might not get any inquiry—so don't count too much on it."

"I'll try to forget about it," Margie said, "and enjoy the circus while I can."

"But you're not getting the full benefit of circus experience," Red teased. "No sloshing around in muddy lots. No soggy clothes that won't get dry during a week of rain. Not a storm this season."

Margie crossed her fingers. "Don't say that," she said. "Every day has been so warm and sunny—you don't have to ask for trouble."

He laughed. "You *are* picking up the superstitions of the circus," he said. "And you're doing better every day with the elephants. You're becoming a real performer, Margie."

They had almost reached the circus lot. Strung out before the Big Top were the show banners, bigger than life-sized paintings in bright blue and yellow, of a gipsy-like woman with her rock python wrapped around her neck, a family of tight-wire walkers, the snarling head of an orange and black striped tiger, an elephant with a lady in pink riding high in its trunk.

Margie liked the smell of the sweet pink candy floss

74

which the white coated concession men sold through the audience during performances, and of hot dogs cooking on a grill. She had even grown accustomed to the odors of the animal cages.

"I'll hate to leave," she said, "if I do find out who I am."

"Well, I don't think it's going to be today," Red said. "I'm hungry. Let's get a hot dog before practice."

Eating a hot dog, Margie went to the kraal where the elephants were tethered, ringed only by a rope to keep careless people from coming too near. Dolly had finished her practice and was ready to teach Margie more of the act they were preparing.

"We sent the picture," Margie said as she placed a foot carefully against Lizzie's trunk. She had learned that an elephant, for all its size, had a very sensitive skin. She must be careful.

Dolly said nothing. She had not been in favor of sending a picture to the newspaper. "It might bring crank letters from undesirable persons," she had objected. She had agreed only after Leo pointed out that Margie had a right to know who she was, and, so far, they weren't learning much.

Standing on Lizzie's back, Margie could see far across the wide Wisconsin pastures edged with woods and blue lakes. Then she looked down at the other four elephants in the kraal. They swayed gently on their enormous legs and tossed hay into their mouths with their trunks.

Mammoth Peewee was probably named for the size of her brain, Margie thought. As usual she was squealing jealously because a bull hand was feeding another elephant first. Peewee pulled at her tether and stole the hay from the more patient one.

Lizzie lifted her trunk and trumpeted a warning. Peewee settled down.

Margie thought how frightened she had been the first time Lizzie trumpeted like that when she was on the old elephant's back. Now she knelt between the great ears and patted the sand-papery hide. She had grown fond of the old leader and trusted her.

"Stand with one leg stretched before you," Dolly called to Margie. "Now your shoulders back—gives your body a better line. That's right."

When Margie was posed correctly, Lizzie shuffled slowly around the kraal. The old elephant was accustomed to this but Margie was excited.

Tonight for the first time, she was to ride in the grand finale. Her costume and Lizzie's matching blanket were ready. She would hold the flag of the United States high above her head while the band played a medley of patriotic songs.

The sun went down red against a murky sky as the performers lined up in the backyard behind the Big Top and waited for their entrances. Everyone chattered and rushed around as usual except Margie who found there was a knot in her stomach. The roof of her mouth was dry. She couldn't say a word.

Her short red, white and blue suit fit well. Her tall striped hat with its white plume was snug over her light brown hair. She had on just enough makeup to appear natural under the bright lights. But she felt sure that a seam would split when she bowed, or her hat would fall off; something would go wrong.

Toomai, standing beside Lizzie, looked at the sky. "Lizzie restless, smell rain," he said to himself, for he never spoke directly to Margie.

Darkness came. The acts whizzed by inside in the ring. Margie heard the clapping, the shouts and the laughter. Sweat broke out in the palms of her hands. Those were people in there. They would all be watching her. If she dropped the flag, or slipped from Lizzie's back—.

"Time to go," Toomai called without looking at Margie.

There was no one to help her now. Dolly, Leo, Red and Sally were all attending to their own parts in the finale. In a daze Margie stood before Lizzie. The old elephant lifted her trunk and touched the girl's shoulder delicately. She seemed to be saying, everything will be all right.

She lowered her trunk and curled the end. Margie braced a foot against it and rode to the top of her head. The band played "Yankee Doodle." Lizzie took off. She was not shuffling as she did in practice.

The moment the spotlight picked them up at the door, the old elephant responded with a brisk pace, lifting her enormous legs daintily and surely, as if she shed years because it was the thing to do. Here was her audience. They must be pleased. She would give them what they wanted to see. She seemed to be trying to tell Margie something the girl must understand about show business.

The old elephant's professional ease brought Margie out of her stage-fright. She looked out over the blur of faces, held the flag high and sang from pure joy. No one could hear her above the band and the tramp of animals parading around inside the Big Top. She sang "America" and "It's a Grand Old Flag."

People clapped. They clapped for everyone, but they clapped especially for Margie and Lizzie as they went by.

When the show was over and Lizzie swung her to the ground in the backyard, Margie gave the old elephant's trunk a quick pat. "You were wonderful, Lizzie."

"So were you," Red called.

Sally was with him. Dolly and Leo came, too. Everyone told her how well she had done. She tried to seem modest about her achievement but this was a night she would remember all her life.

And for more than one reason. She was leaving the wardrobe tent when a flash of lightning forked overhead followed by a deep rumble of thunder. A cold gust of wind chilled the warm night air.

"Margie," Sally said, "your opening night brought us the first storm of the season."

"It figgers," Red said. Even in the dark she knew he was grinning. Then his voice changed. "Run. The storm's coming fast, and it's cold enough for hail."

Before Margie could reach the trailer, icy pellets cut her bare arms and legs. Dolly and Leo ran beside her. Leo had to slam the trailer door twice and hold his back against it, the wind was so strong. Rain and hail beat a loud tattoo on the aluminum roof.

"I'm going to my cats," Leo shouted over the din. "They'll be wild in this storm. Maybe I can quiet them."

"The elephants, too," Dolly cried, ready to go, too.

He stopped her. "No one can do a thing if elephants

decide to stampede." He went out the door, turned and came back. "Don't leave this trailer until I come for you," he said. "Tree limbs are blowing through camp like tumble weeds and the electric light line just went down."

Margie and Dolly ran to the trailer windows and tried to see the elephant kraal when shimmers of lightning opened the darkness. The huge beasts were huddled together, their tails to the wind. But nothing could protect their sensitive skin from the hail which beat upon them.

In a brilliant flash of lightning, the elephants ap-

peared for a moment to be enormous swaying pictures done in black on a silver screen. They fanned their ears in fright and rolled their trunks to protect the tender snouts.

Lightning burned the sky and a crash of thunder shook the trailer. Margie caught Dolly's hand as the elephants squealed and trumpeted. One of them broke loose from her tether.

"Peewee, I'll bet," Margie cried.

The elephant was running. She crashed straight through the women's dressing tent. Then there was a rumble more terrible than thunder, the sound of many enormous feet moving past the trailer. All five elephants were loose.

"Stampeding," Dolly said.

She ran to the door and opened it. Margie ducked under her arm to watch, too.

The hail had passed. Torrents of rain continued. Wind whipped the soaked clothing of men scurrying around the backyard. They had turned on the headlights of all the cars and trucks. Some of the men carried flashlights as well.

Toomai ran out in front of Lizzie who stopped. He waved his flashlight and shouted orders to the bull hands who were trying to round up the scattered elephants.

Finally, all the elephants grew quiet at the men's familiar commands except Peewee. She acted as if she had wanted to do what she was doing for a long time, and now had a fine excuse.

Peewee smashed through the yard tearing down the pony fence and the ponies fled before her. She tipped over the cage of monkeys who screamed insults after her. She ran her trunk through the window of the Cunningham's trailer and brought out a pillow which she tore into shreds, then stamped beneath her feet. She was on her way to the cookhouse when Lizzie took out after her.

Lizzie trumpeted her outrage, a clear command for Peewee to stop. But the rampaging elephant smashed through the kitchen, tossing pots and pans into the air like a juggler.

Then Peewee came out and looked about for her next target, her trunk swinging from side to side angrily. Lizzie faced her and trumpeted. The huge young elephant refused to obey. She lifted her trunk and trumpeted defiantly. She seemed to say, stop me if you can.

Toomai ran toward them, his arms lifted above his head, calling something. He looked ant-size against their great bulk. Peewee flung up her trunk and started for him.

Margie's hand went to her throat. An elephant's trunk could choke a man in seconds.

Suddenly, neatly, Lizzie put out a huge leg and tripped Peewee, sending her forward upon her knees. Peewee slid through the water and mud until she came up against Kate, whom a bull hand had brought up quickly.

Lizzie followed. As Peewee struggled to her feet, the old elephant shouldered her against Kate. Between them, Lizzie and Kate squeezed Peewee until she was subdued and they took her back to the kraal. Quickly the bull hands tethered them to their iron stakes.

Margie did not know she had been holding her breath, until she looked at Dolly and they smiled in relief.

"I wonder if Toomai will remember Lizzie's reward in all this excitement," Margie said. "I hope he still has some peanuts or a bottle of coke for her."

CHAPTER SEVEN

To Save Lizzie

In the morning the sun shone hot again. Everyone worked to clean up after the storm. The Big Top had little damage, for the men had let it to the ground and tied it down during the storm. The dressing tents were sagging and torn. Performers went around picking up costumes from the grass and from trees.

Margie held up her muddy red, white and blue costume which she found wrapped around an overturned tub. Sally and Red waved to her.

"How will we ever put on a performance tomorrow night?" Margie called.

"Lucky today's Sunday," Sally said as she and Red joined Margie.

"We'll manage," Red said. "We always have."

Margie saw then that the backyard was already as busy as an ants' hill when someone has disturbed their home. Women were rinsing clothes in rainwater found in every bucket. Men were driving stakes, sewing up canvas, repairing the cooktent.

The elephants were doing the heavy work, commanded by Toomai and the bull hands. They lifted and straightened center tent poles which had fallen. With their foreheads they pushed trucks mired hub-deep in the muddy field. They pulled an overturned trailer into place. Old as she was, Lizzie seemed to do most of the work for she knew how to do it. She always had to begin a task before the other elephants would follow.

The cleanup continued all day although the heat grew almost unbearable. By supper time Margie could not think of food. She ought to be hungry but she only longed for a bath. Hot water in a real bathtub, with bubble oil, and afterwards flower-scented powder.

She frowned. She must have had that kind of bath some place to want it now.

"Come on!" Red shouted to her. "Let's swim in the lake across the pasture if you can walk that far."

It seemed a long way, Margie thought, but the lake water did look cool. She went with Sally and Red. They were almost through the pasture when Margie glanced back and saw Lizzie following them. She was alone, shuffling slowly.

TO SAVE LIZZIE

"Look," Margie said, "Lizzie's coming with us. How did she get away from the other elephants?"

"She probably just quit work to go swimming," Red said, "like we did."

"She loves the water," Sally added, "and she's worked terribly hard today."

"She's walking so slowly," Margie said. "There, she stumbled."

The young people turned and waited. Lizzie was barely dragging her enormous feet now. She stumbled again and went down on her front knees. She struggled to stand, but could not. She lifted her trunk as if she wanted to trumpet her frustration, but no sound came. Her head leaned and she went over on her side.

For a moment Margie did not know what to think. Elephants did lie down when they were tired. But no crumpling up this way, and not in the middle of a pasture on the way to water.

Red moved first. Margie and Sally were close behind him when they reached Lizzie who lay on her side looking oddly helpless for all her bulk. The long straight lashes were closed over her little eyes.

Red said. "She's exhausted. She could be sick. We'll never get her back to the kraal unless she can walk. I'll get the doctor." He ran.

Margie didn't know what to do. She saw the elephant's big ribs rise and fall with her breathing. At least Lizzie was alive. "Maybe she needs something to eat," she suggested.

Sally picked and brought fresh clover in the swim towel she was carrying to the lake. "She knows your voice best, Margie," Sally said. "You'd better try to feed her."

Margie approached the elephant quietly. Lizzie had curled her trunk on top of her tree-stump sized legs. Margie knew the power in that trunk if Lizzie lashed out in her fright or pain.

She wished she knew what Toomai said in his Indian tongue when he soothed the elephants. She kept saying as she moved closer, "There, there, Lizzie." She held out a handful of clover.

The end of the sensitive trunk quivered, moved slowly, hovered above the clover, then passed by.

Margie coaxed, "You like sweet clover. It'll make you stronger."

The elephant did not move again, and Margie was troubled. Her first fear of the elephant had changed to liking and trust. She wanted Lizzie to live, but she knew of nothing to do except to stand beside the great head, so Lizzie would know she was not alone.

At last, Sally said. "Red's coming with the doctor and Daddy and Toomai."

Even a man as experienced with animals as the circus doctor, found it difficult to decide what to do for a patient the size of Lizzie.

"She's getting some age on her," he said at last to Mr. Cunningham. "She was cold and wet last night and worked hard today. Rest will help if that is all."

"What else could be wrong?" Mr. Cunningham said.

"She may have eaten something that disagreed with her," the circus doctor said. "She could have picked up anything on that cluttered lot after the storm. We'll give her a dose of oil, cooking oil will do."

Toomai, squatting beside the elephant's head, looked up. "Peewee spill all cooking oil last night," he said.

"Maybe some of our circus people have oil," Mr. Cunningham said.

"We'll need four or five gallons," the doctor said.

"Then I'll go into town and get a grocer or druggist to open his store. I'll get oil somewhere," Mr. Cunningham said and hurried away across the field.

The doctor looked at the sun going down. "Evenings grow chilly here," he said. "We can't risk her getting pneumonia. We'll want a couple of low fires, one a little distance from her back, one to keep her feet warm. If Lizzie's knees get so stiff she can't get on her feet, then she's a goner. Nothing we can do to get her up. Think you kids can find plenty of dead wood?"

Red, Sally and Margie started for the trees nearby to

pick up fallen branches. "We'll need a lot to feed two bonfires all night," Red said.

They carried armfuls of wood until it was too dark to gather more. When they returned with their last load, a small group of people had gathered around Lizzie. The grocer, who had opened his store to get five gallons of oil, had come with Mr. Cunningham to see if he could help. The fire and police chiefs came from the town. They agreed that it was safe to build small bonfires here in the open pasture.

One of the bull hands came with blankets to lay over Lizzie's knees. Men laid the fires and Red struck a match to them. Everything had been done that could be done.

Mr. Cunningham said, "Time for you kids to be in bed. We have a long drive tomorrow."

"Tomorrow?" Margie asked. "We won't go unless Lizzie is better, will we?"

Toomai looked at her in surprise. Margie was dirty and scratched and so tired her eyelids were swollen, but she was thinking of Lizzie.

"Doctor and I stay with Lizzie," Toomai said, "you not worry."

It was the first time that Toomai had ever spoken to Margie as if she were a part of the circus and not a stranger. She felt better as she walked home with Red and Sally.

The next morning right after breakfast the circus trailers and trucks were ready to roll. Lizzie and the doctor and Toomai were still in the pasture. Mr. Cunningham said the circus must move, but he would leave an elephant truck and driver to bring Lizzie later if she could get on her feet.

"If?" Margie said to him. "Lizzie *will* be all right, won't she?"

"I surely hope so," he said, "but we can't wait to see. We have a performance to give tonight." He turned and waved to his drivers. "Everyone aboard—and away!"

That night Margie watched from the performers' entrance as the acts followed one another in the center of the Big Top. There was the usual bowing, smiling, slapping and laughter. How could they, when nothing was the same without Lizzie?

Then she learned something more about circus people. They were gay before the audience, but the performers understood how Margie felt. As they left the tent, they stopped one by one and spoke to her. Mr. Carter let his tiny dog sniff her hair and bark until she managed a smile. Nell, with her python wrapped around her neck and arm, brought Margie an ice cream cone.

"Lizzie will be along in a day or so, you'll see," Nell comforted her.

The third morning, Margie was wakened by the sound of a truck pulling into the backyard, turning, backing. She looked from the window and saw the elephant truck which had been left behind. Was it empty? Or had Lizzie recovered?

The driver stepped from the cab and opened the back of the truck. Bull hands came running to put a heavy ramp in place. Lizzie placed an enormous foot cautiously on the ramp and came down.

Margie jumped from her bed, pulled on her shorts and blouse and ran to meet her elephant. She wiped her cheek with her arm as she saw Lizzie enter the kraal where all the elephants surrounded her, touching her with their trunks, welcoming her.

"They're actually telling Lizzie how glad they are to see her," Margie said to Toomai who stood beside the kraal.

"They feel better—their leader back," he said.

"They are all stronger than Lizzie now," Margie said. "Will they still follow and obey her?"

"A leader not have to be strongest," Toomai said. "She lead because her judgment good. She fair and patient and wise. They trust her. *That* makes a leader."

CHAPTER EIGHT

They Are Out There

For Margie the weeks passed swiftly as the circus moved fifty to a hundred miles daily and played a new town each night. She began to feel that she had never known any life but this one of tearing down tents, loading, traveling.

She felt at home walking along the one main street in the backyard of the circus between rows of animals and rows of living-tents and trailers. Music, costumes, laughter, lights, people and applause. She performed every night now and she knew her act was good.

One evening, as Margie waited with Red and Sally outside the Big Top between performances, she said, "We've never had an answer to our advertisement, so I guess I'll always stay with the circus."

"You really like it now, don't you?" Red sounded pleased.

Margie nodded.

"You sure have changed," Sally said.

"Yes," Margie agreed, "But it took me long enough to learn the act."

"I don't mean only the act," Sally said. "You've changed in other ways. You don't look at Nell and Toomai as if they were freaks anymore."

"Sally!" Red said with his usual groan at his sister's frankness.

"Well, you know she did when she first came," Sally said to him.

She looked up at Margie high on Lizzie's head. "You're much nicer now, Margie. You even used to stare at Red and me as if we were somehow different from other people—not quite human—because we walked a tight-wire for a living."

For a moment Margie was angry, then she knew that Sally was right. She had looked upon most circus people as somehow foreign, to be feared a little. But she had found them warm and friendly, much kinder to a stranger than she had any right to expect.

"Well, I don't think so now," she said. "I've learned a lot this summer."

Lizzie curled her trunk and touched Margie's ankle.

THEY ARE OUT THERE

It was time for their act and they entered the Big Top through the curtained door at the back of the ring.

Red was waiting for Margie when she came from the women's dressing tent after the show. He often walked home with her through the half-dark street. They liked talking together about funny things that happened back-stage, or about people, or about something they had read or heard on the radio. In fact, they just liked walking and talking together, Margie thought.

"What's bothering you?" Red asked now.

"Are you a mind-reader?" Margie asked. "What makes you think something is bothering me?"

"You've been pretty quiet, for you," he said grinning.

"You know Dolly and Leo are engaged to be married?" she asked.

"I think it's great," he said. "They're two nice people!"

"That's just it," Margie said. "Do you think they're putting off their wedding because Dolly has me to look after?"

"No," he said definitely. "They want to be married when they reach winter quarters, when they can take a few weeks off. Our tour will be over in a couple of months."

"I feel better," she said, "for they've gone to a lot of expense and trouble for a stranger."

They had reached the trailer and saw Dolly and Leo seated in lawn chairs beside it. Their backs were toward her and Margie was about to call, "Hi", when she heard what Dolly was saying:

"I can't believe Margie is any relation to that man."

"I don't like the sound of his letter either," Leo answered. "But Father Kelly must have thought R. R. Klasner *might* be her uncle, or he wouldn't have sent the letter on to us."

Margie stood very still. It wasn't that she wanted to eavesdrop. She simply could not speak.

"This man is only anxious to find a missing heir so an estate can be settled and he can get his share," Dolly said.

Red took hold of Margie's hand, as if he understood how disturbed she was.

"But if he is Margie's uncle," Leo said, "we haven't any choice but to let him come and see her."

"I could give her up to someone who really loved her," Dolly argued.

"As you do?" Leo said gently.

Dolly nodded.

"I knew *you'd* help *her*," Leo said. "I hadn't counted on Margie's helping you so much."

"She's helped me become myself again, after losing Linda," Dolly said. "She gave me something else to think of besides my grief."

Quickly Margie went to her. "I hope I have," she said, "you've gone to so much trouble for me—with no real reason to. I—"

Dolly hugged her. "It's worthwhile even to make *one* person happy," she said. "We managed to make things better for *two*."

"I haven't found you too hard to have around either," Red said to her, then frowned. "What about this Klasner? Did I bring his inquiry with the ad and my snapshot?"

"No," Leo said. "A newspaper reporter wrote a feature story about the fire which was picked up by the press across the country. He stated there were still several unidentified dead. He also told about Father Kelly rescuing child after child from the burning Big Top. Klasner's a farmer in Iowa. He read the story and wrote to Father Kelly asking if he knew anything about the unclaimed persons."

"Klasner wants to find his brother's daughter, an orphan placed in a home near Hartford. She'd be about your age," Dolly added. "Of course he hadn't bothered to look for his niece in years, not until the girl has to be found so his brother's estate can be settled."

"Is he coming here?" Margie asked.

"Not until he gets his hogs to market," Dolly said. "He wrote that he had our schedule and we'd be nearer Iowa next week."

"The generous type," Red said. "Who needs him?"

"Please," Margie said. "He just can't be my uncle. Do I have to go with him?"

"Not unless he has absolute proof, you don't," Dolly said. "Try not to think about it. Father Kelly is investigating in Hartford."

"And the whole circus will look after you here," Red said.

"Don't worry," Leo said, "If you're not Ida Klasner, you won't go with him."

"I can't be," Margie said again, "but what if I am?"

"Let's cross that bridge when and if we come to it," Dolly said. "Right now we should go to bed. We move early in the morning."

At breakfast Margie sat down at the table with Red and Sally in the half-filled cookhouse. She could hear tent men next door rolling canvas to hoist onto a trailer. Today they would travel another hundred miles nearer Iowa and a man who claimed to be her uncle but had been too unconcerned for ten years to find her.

"I feel my name is Margie," she said, pouring syrup on the pancakes Red got for her.

"Margie *what?*" Sally urged.

"I don't know!" Margie said. "The doctor told us that I might remember in fragments, bit by bit. Then one day I might remember everything as if I had just waked from a dream."

Red nodded. "I don't know the medical reasons," he said, "but I read an article at the dentist's when I had a tooth filled last week. One of the magazines on his shelf had an explanation of amnesia. The mind blocks out something too painful to remember. A person recovers when she gets rested or stronger or from some shock, like meeting face to face with a person she loved or was afraid of or—"

"It should be shock enough," Sally said, "to think you might be Ida Klasner."

Margie said nothing. After a moment's silence, Red said, "I wish now I hadn't sent that ad and snapshot to the newspaper. If you're not Ida, we might get another answer like Klasner's."

"I wonder if the picture was printed," Sally said. "A month and we've never heard a word."

The tent men began taking down the cookhouse. The three young people ran to the waiting trailers to travel with their families. It was long past noon when Dolly drove into the circus lot on the outskirts of a town. The animals were already in their tents or kraals, for the roustabouts, cage boys and bull hands had loaded the animals at night and left hours ahead of the performers.

"Lucky we don't have a matinee," Dolly said. "I'm going to take advantage of the free time and shampoo my hair. How about you?"

"I'm hungry," Margie said. "I'll get an ice cream cone first."

She found Red and Sally at the refrigerator car eating chocolate ice cream cones. While she waited for hers, a passenger train roared by, its whistle shrieking.

"Wow," Red said when it had passed, "what a place for the circus grounds, right beside the main line. You better watch Lizzie tonight."

Margie smiled. She had lost her fear of Lizzie weeks ago. Together, she and the old elephant paraded as the show opened, and performed their butterfly act in the finale.

"I'll see you later," Margie said. "Dolly and I are going to give each other shampoos."

Margie's shining brown hair had grown below her earlobes now. When it was washed, she walked behind the tents, fluffing her wet hair with her hands so the sun would dry it. She came to the train tracks and walked the railroad ties.

Late summer is beautiful, she thought, bright yellow goldenrod and sunflowers. And this time of day when the sun is low, the sky seems bluer, the grass greener and the new-cut hay smells sweeter than at any other time.

She did not hear Red and Sally until they were right beside her.

"Were you hard to find!" Red exclaimed.

100

She was surprised to see him here. Red and his father usually checked the rigging and props before supper, to be sure the riggers had tightened each correctly.

"You're not going to believe this," Sally said trying to talk and catch her breath at the same time, "but a man says you are his daughter."

Margie just looked at them.

"It never rains but it pours," Red added with a smile that he meant to be reassuring. "This time it's an answer to our ad."

"He called Daddy this afternoon from a way station," Sally said. "He's coming here now by train."

"Who?" Margie cried.

"Thomas Manning," Red said, "the man who says he's your father."

"Manning," Margie said to herself, "Margie Manning." It did not mean a thing.

"Don't you recognize your own name, even when you hear it?" Sally asked.

Margie shook her head.

"Then maybe you *are* Ida Klasner," Sally wailed.

Red spoke earnestly. "My father asked Mr. Manning a lot of questions and he had some convincing answers. Dad's pretty sure he's your father."

"Where is your father?" Margie asked, hoping that Mr. Cunningham could tell her more.

101

"Talking to Dolly" Red answered. "He thought she should be the one to tell you."

"But we found you first," Sally said.

"If this man who telephoned is my father," Margie asked, "why has he waited all this time to find me?"

"He said he had been away all summer on a trip deep into the rainforests of South America with pack mules, where no mail could reach him. He didn't have letters for months or see newspapers until he reached his home in New York City yesterday."

"What in the world was he doing in the jungle?" Margie asked.

Red hesitated. "He said he left right after his wedding. He and his wife had gone on a digging seminar to study ancient Mayan culture. It sounds—as if you had a new stepmother, Margie, just before you lost your memory."

"Maybe it wasn't the fire," Sally said excitedly. "Maybe you didn't like her. Maybe you wanted to forget—"

Red interrupted. "Anyway they came home yesterday and found a letter from a friend of your father's—of Mr. Manning's. The friend enclosed our ad and picture from the Hartford paper, and said the girl looked so much like his daughter that he sent it on, in case the girl might be related to him. Your father recognized

102

you at once and got right on the train. After he made a few phone calls."

Margie could not have been more stunned if they had told her that a tiger had broken loose and was coming for her. "I don't remember him. I won't recognize him."

"Did you have an Aunt Sarah?" Sally asked abruptly.

Red explained quickly, "Mr. Manning said he telephoned to an Aunt Sarah in Maine to see what she knew. She thought you were on a camping trip with friends named Ross. And she was pretty provoked because you had not written to her."

"Then your father called the Ross family," Sally added. "They thought you had gone to your Aunt Sarah's when Susanna Ross got measles and their trip had to be cancelled. So did the principal of your school."

Margie was only more bewildered.

Red saw that she was near tears. He began to walk back to Dolly's trailer with her. "Maybe R. R. Klasner and Thomas Manning are both false alarms," he said. "Not much we can do but eat supper and get on with the show, and see what happens when this Mr. Manning does get here."

Dolly and Leo agreed when Margie told them what Red had said.

"His train gets in here about the time the show

103

opens," Leo added. "Mr. Manning said he would take a taxi to the circus grounds."

"At least," Dolly said, "He lost no time in coming. He must love you very much."

Margie saw that Dolly seemed convinced that this man might be her father. But Margie was not. Wouldn't she remember him after all that information?

She was still doubtful that evening as she waited in her place for the opening parade of animals and performers to enter the Big Top. She wore a new yellow costume with gauzy butterfly wings, and Lizzie wore a matching gold satin blanket. She should feel happy, but she only felt that this was all a mistake. In a very short time, she would meet a disappointed stranger.

The band struck up the music, and she saw Red and Sally running toward her. What were they doing here? Dressed in their brief sparkling costumes, they should be in the line of parade.

"*They* are out there," Red said.

"They?" Margie questioned.

"Your father and his wife," Red said. "They just got here. The gateman brought them to our trailer. My father is having them seated out there now, in guest seats right above the show's director."

"Your father said he didn't want to spoil your act," Sally said. "He'll watch, and see you after the show."

It was all happening too fast. "I don't believe he's my father," she cried.

The tent's curtains opened into the performing ring. "We've got to run," Red said, then turned. "He says your name *is* Margie."

Toomai appeared, his tall turban quivering in his exasperation. "Up, up," he shouted. "Line is moving."

Lizzie lifted Margie onto her wide head and jogged into the spotlight at the entrance to the Big Top. Margie spread her gauzy golden wings and turned slowly on the toes of her ballet slippers. She must not look toward the guest seats or she might make a mistake. She had worked hard to perfect this act and everyone was watching her.

In no time at all, the parade had circled the inside of the tent. As she passed the director, Margie dared to look at the upturned faces in the audience. Under the spotlights, they all looked alike. Then a tall man half-rose from his seat and waved to her, a mixture of joy and relief in his smile.

Something hard and unyielding seemed to shatter in her chest. She said, "Daddy, Daddy." No one could hear her above the band music but she waved, blinking and smiling.

Then she saw a slender woman, with ash-blond hair, seated beside her father, the woman waved and smiled, too. A rush of anger made Margie feel warm all over. She lost her balance and grabbed for Lizzie's head strap as the opening parade left the Bip Top.

How she hated that woman who had married her father and taken him off on a honeymoon for the entire summer. Until now Margie and her father had spent their summer vacations together at his Aunt Sarah's home on an island off the coast of Maine.

"I do have an Aunt Sarah," Margie said aloud. "The gray kitten was at her house. I'm remembering everything."

Her life had been good until her father met Anne Syme, an archeologist, who taught in a University near New York City where her father was dean of men. Right after their wedding, her father and his wife had gone off on a digging seminar deep in the jungles of Guatemala.

"I have to learn to hack my way through steaming rain-forests with a machette," her father had told Margie and laughed.

He had taken her by the shoulders then and added earnestly, "You were too young to remember your mother, Margie. But it's good to have a mother. When we return in the fall, I hope you'll feel differently about Anne. She's a very nice person. You'll like her if you give her a chance."

"I never will," Margie wept now as she reached the backyard and slid off Lizzie's head.

Red and Sally ran along the line to meet her. "Did you see them?" Red asked.

She nodded. They waited a minute for her to tell them more, but she could say nothing.

"Your father is distinguished appearing," Sally said. "Your mother looks nice, too."

"She's not my mother," Margie cried. "She's not even the person I want for a mother. She's odd. Her idea of a honeymoon was to visit some ancient Mayan tomb-chamber, she calls it—and study hieroglyphic writings on the walls there. And she made my father go with her."

Red and Sally looked startled by her outburst. Margie realized she was not being exactly fair. Her father had *wanted* to go, and his wife had planned the trip long before she married him. It was a field trip to complete her doctorate degree.

Red stared at Margie with a puzzled frown. "You act like you're afraid of her," he said. "Daddy says that's what hate is—fear of someone. When we're afraid they'll take something from us."

"You don't like her because she took your father away from you," Sally said.

"She did not," Margie said. "No one could do that.

My father and I always do everything together. We—"

She stopped. Sally had spoken the truth. She had been afraid, and terribly jealous that this woman would take her father's time and affection from her.

"Everyone loves more than one person," Sally said. "I love all my family."

"It's time for our act," Red urged. "Come on, Sally." They ran.

Margie stood beside Lizzie and watched her trunk sway back and forth to the music of the band. Every other performer in the line was absorbed in his part of the show, and Margie had time to think.

Facts fell into place in her mind until she remembered all that had happened the day she started to go to Aunt Sarah's in Maine, the same day she went to see the circus, the same day that she woke and did not know who she was. She felt just as if she were seeing a play with another girl who looked like her, but was not Margie as she had become this summer living with the circus.

Her father and she had lived in a small apartment in New York City. After a succession of housekeepers, her father had decided that she was better off during the school year in a girls' boarding school in Connecticut. She had looked forward to her holidays and summers with him.

Then in June he married and she was expected to

spend her vacation alone in Maine with Great-Aunt Sarah after school closed.

"You like Maine," Margie's roommate, Susanna Ross, had said.

"Not without Father," Margie had said. "Aunt Sarah won't even let me take the boat out without him there. There'll be nothing to do."

"Then come camping with us," Susanna had said. "I'd love to have you, so would Mother and Dad."

She had telephoned to her father in New York and he agreed to her change of plans. He had said, "I'll call Aunt Sarah and tell her you're going with the Ross'. We leave tomorrow ourselves, Anne and I. Have a good summer, Margie."

She might have had, but at the last moment when everything was packed, and she was the last girl to leave the school, Mrs. Ross had telephoned. Susanna had come down with the measles, their trip was cancelled, indefinitely, for the two younger children would probably have measles, too.

"I'm sorry about Susanna," Margie had said, trying not to show her own feeling of disappointment and loneliness.

"What about you?" Mrs. Ross had asked. "Will you go to your Aunt Sarah's?"

"Yes," Margie had said, "I'll be all right." As right as anyone could be who was hurt and angry, she thought.

She telephoned Aunt Sarah but no one answered. It was ten o'clock. Everyone on the island went to the post office in the village at midmorning when the boat brought the mail.

Margie would have to hurry to catch the noon train from Hartford. She could call Aunt Sarah from the station there. She had gone to the school office and found no one in at the moment. Most of the staff was on vacation. Margie had left a note giving her change of summer address at Aunt Sarah's, although she probably would not receive mail with her father so far from civilization.

She would need nothing at Aunt Sarah's except the things she had already packed in one bag for the camping trip. She walked down the driveway to the main road and waited for a bus which would take her to the railroad station in Hartford. From a phone booth she had called Aunt Sarah. Again there was no answer. Aunt Sarah must be in the garden. She never could hear the telephone out there. Margie would just have to surprise her by her arrival.

Then she had seen the colored circus poster on the wall: See the GREATEST SHOW ON EARTH, July 6, 1944.

Today, Margie had thought. I'd love to see it. And why not? I have my allowance. Aunt Sarah's not expecting me. I can catch the first train after the circus.

She had gone to the circus. The fire in the Big Top and her loss of memory had decided the summer for her. But not her real problem.

The summer is over, Margie thought. I know who I am now. My father and his wife are in the Big Top waiting to see me as soon as the show ends.

Margie cupped her face in her hands. She had been disagreeable and self-centered about her father's marriage. She thought she had changed so much this summer, and she had. Anne Syme, Anne Manning now, no longer seemed odd because she spent her vacations studying hieroglyphics in a Mayan Chamber.

Still Margie did not like her father's wife. She just could not like her.

Suddenly she felt an arm go around her. It was Dolly on her way to the Big Top.

"Margie," she said, "I met your father and mother. I went to their seats a moment before the show began. They're nice. I'm happy for you."

She kissed the girl's cheek and ran to do her act. Margie watched her go.

She would be happy for me, Margie thought. Dolly might have pitied herself so much that she couldn't bear to look at another girl Linda's age. Yet she took me in and treated me like her daughter. Dear, kind, thoughtful Dolly.

Margie felt Lizzie's trunk circle her waist. Everyone

111

was pushing into line for the finale. It was time to move.

She rode into the Big Top on the fast-paced, delicately high-stepping, old elephant. The house lights were dimmed. A spotlight picked them up at the entrance and followed them wherever they went. Margie saw that her golden ballet slippers pointed elegantly. The folds of her yellow net tutu stood out stiff and crisp from her slender waist.

Finally Lizzie stopped in the center, lifted Margie in her trunk and held her high. The girl looked out over the up-turned faces and heard indrawn breaths of pleasure when she spread her gauzy wings while the band played, "Beautiful Butterfly."

The two golden antennas, secured with a ribbon band in her long brown hair, remained in place. Everything went perfectly, but there was a peculiar heavy feeling in Margie's stomach. This was probably her last performance in a circus.

Lizzie curled Margie in her trunk, stood on her hind legs, her enormous front legs hanging like a puppy's begging for a bone, and waited for the audience to applaud. When the clapping came, she tossed Margie onto her head, spread her great fan ears, trumpeted her "thank-you" to the people, and pranced out of the spotlight.

Around the track once more they went in a parade of

all the performers while the band played the "Star Spangled Banner."

Then the show was over. Margie found herself in the backyard standing beside the old elephant, hugging her trunk, blinking rapidly.

"You were wonderful," Sally said as she and Red reached Margie's side.

"Your father should be proud," Red added.

"I am," Margie heard her father say.

It had not taken him long to find his way through the Big Top. He hugged her. She smelled the pine shaving lotion he had always used. This was her own father and she was overjoyed to be with him again.

Then Margie saw her father's wife standing a little apart. Her gray eyes shone with the hope of sharing her husband and Margie's happiness.

Margie thought in astonishment, she's the stranger in our family, as much a stranger as I was in the circus. What had Dolly said to her about making someone happy? "It's worthwhile to make even one person happy, and we managed to make life better for *two!*"

Margie felt that some of Dolly's kindness must have rubbed off on her. She was actually beginning to understand that her stepmother had a problem, too. She wanted Margie to accept her. Now Margie saw that she had a chance to make *three* persons happy: her father, his wife, and maybe herself. She managed a smile for

114

Anne Manning. "I hope your summer was as much fun as mine," she said.

Her father looked pleased. Her mother came to them and said, "We found a larger apartment, Margie, not far from a good high school. We hope you'll want to live at home with us now."

"I'd like that," Margie said.

"Where's Mrs. Vasi?" her father asked, "I owe her many thanks."

"Dolly's dressing," Margie said, "I'll have to change, too. Will you wait outside the dressing tent for us?"

"Lead the way," he said and walked with his wife behind the three young people.

Red was quiet. Margie looked at him. "We'll miss you," he said.

"And I'll miss you," Margie said.

Sally turned and walked backwards, speaking to Mr. Manning, "Can Margie come back next summer?"

"We'll see," he answered.

Margie and Red walked a little ahead and he locked the fingers of one hand through hers.

"He'll let me," Margie said. "I'll visit the circus as often as I can."

And she did not mean to watch from the audience in the Big Top, but to visit in the backyard where the real life of the circus went on.